OUTRÉ

Outré

D. HARLAN WILSON

RAW DOG
SCREAMING
PRESS

Outré
Copyright © 2020 by D. Harlan Wilson
ISBN: 978-1-94-787920-1
Library of Congress Control Number: 2020935348

First Paperback Edition, November 2020

Cover Design © 2020 by Brad Sharp
www.bradsharp.co.uk

Author Photo © 2020 by Betty Lomax
www.lomaxphotography.com

Raw Dog Screaming Press
Bowie, MD
www.rawdogscreamingpress.com

Wilson, D. Harlan (b. 1971)
Outré / a novel; sub. "Ablations and Conflagrations"; prelude to *Usurper*
SF / Science Fiction, Speculative Fiction, Superzero Fiction, Surreal Flâneury, Schiz Flow
1. Title 2. Series
1 Kings 16-22 / Genesis 16: 11-12
n - 1 2 3 4 5 6 7 8 9 0

BOOKS BY D. HARLAN WILSON

Novels
Primordial: An Abstraction
The Kyoto Man
Codename Prague
Dr. Identity, or, Farewell to Plaquedemia
Peckinpah: An Ultraviolent Romance
Blankety Blank: A Memoir of Vulgaria

Theory-Fiction
The Psychotic Dr. Schreber

Drama
Jackanape and the Fingermen
Three Plays

Biographies
Hitler: The Terminal Biography
Freud: The Penultimate Biography
Douglass: The Lost Autobiography

Fiction Collections
Natural Complexions
Battle without Honor or Humanity: Volume 2
Battle without Honor or Humanity: Volume 1
Diegeses
They Had Goat Heads
Pseudo-City
Stranger on the Loose
The Kafka Effekt

Film/Literary Criticism
Minority Report
J.G. Ballard
They Live
Technologized Desire: Postcapitalist Science Fiction

For Stan, Grant, and Betty

"By art is created that great Leviathan called a Commonwealth or State—which is but an artificial man."

—Thomas Hobbes, *Leviathan*

"It's too late to play dead. I can only pretend to be alive."

—Starke, *Usurper*

0

Cast. Donny Ennui, Dr. Edmund Parkview, Terra Hipp, Sam Struyk, Perrie Dune, Gene Pain, Barry Hog, Sirius Brain, Copernicus Gall, Søren Kierkegaard, Albert Camus, Abraham the Hebrew, Nikolai Gogol, Michael Lassiter, Will Battle, Conrad Johnson, David Happenstance, Morton Leftbank, Barrymore Steed, Hank Burke, Grace Kelly, James Dean, Jayne Mansfield, Sam Kinison, Randy Savage, Roland Barthes, Edwin de Bruns, Lisa Lopes, Roger Vienna, F.W. Murnau, Princess Diana, P. Woodward Still, Orion Oberon, Ray Whirr, Dr. Otto Dykstra, Natalie Wichita, Abner Person, Lee Simian, Curd, Starke, Dr. J.J. Pickle, Sam Peckinpah, Dustin Hoffman, Sun Tzü, Reginald McZed, Dr. Henry Jekyll, Edward Hyde, Connie Middleton, Travis Doom, Billy Idol, Marlon Brando, Horatio Stubb, Ulysses S. Grant, Mr. Mxyzptlk, Tony Grail, Manfred Mann, Naomi Dare, Dick Frost, Harry Florida Jr., Alabaster Seville, Lucy Florida, Harry Florida Sr., Boris Pachulski, Able Friend, Petra Raleigh, James Curry, Z. Delilah Prong, Bill Frank, Vincent Bison, Charlie Drakkar, Hilda Pill Hance, Chanelle Wagner, Bianca Snyde, Herman Melville, Captain Ahab, Moby Dick, Stanley Kubrick, David Lynch, Dale Rigueur, Oprah Winfrey, Lew Wasserman, Ronald Reagan, Vernon Winfrey, Jerry Brown, Kamala Harris, Dianne Feinstein, Paul Marsack, James Bond, Clytemnestra Bol, Lee Blanc, Anais Watterson, Barton Heck, Gary the Cervix, Ludwig van Beethoven, Alexander DeLarge, Kalypso "Ipso" Shadrach, Anthony Hopkins Alt., Nathanial Poe, Daniel-Day Lewis, William Poole, Leonardo Dicaprio,

Victor Bleep, August Eggman, Solomon Israel, Chester Sprague, Adeline Sprague, Dr. Reverend Donovan Ogg Esq., Sally Code, S. Tor Resartus, David Iain Smith, Parker Banshee, Finnegan Wake, Dave Elsey, Benicio del Toro, Carmen Adagio, Tony the Femur, Barbara Winfrey, Barack Obama, Michelle Obama, Ira Überstein, Gary Indiana, Vic Armstrong, Buff Brady, Bob Bralver, Roger Creed, Dick Crockett, Frankie Darro, Babe Defreest, Duke Green, Billy Hank Hooker, Buster Keaton, Eddie Kidd, Bert LeBaron, Jock Mahoney, Bronco McLoughlin, Eddie Polo, Dar Robinson, Guy Teague, Buddy Van Horn, Dale Van Sickel, Dick Warlock, Werner Herzog, Klaus Kinski, Jimmy Stewart, Alfred Hitchcock, John Wayne, John Ford, Johnny Depp, Tim Burton, Gretel Amino, Tom Hanks, Ron Howard, Robert De Niro, Martin Scorsese, Veronica Yen, Cory Finger, Orestes Dirge, King Kong, Charles Darwin, Tiffany Anaconda, Sam Raimi, Ferdinand Kovich, Miriam Shay, Wiley Rant, Baron Caulfield, Jonah of Amittai, Gretel Marcuse, Krysta Now, Liz Taylor, Marilyn Monroe, Sarah Bernhardt, Billy Combs, Widget Moon, Franklin Bolanderos, Sherry Interlaken, Quinn Plotinus Smith, Sanju K., Jack DeLorean VII, Harvey Seigel, Elizabeth Partwater, Fiona Candelabra, Ned Fix, Augustus August, Eddy Caledonia, Lloyd Radar, and Edgar Allan Poe.

1

Nobody. Despite the vitality of my off-color performances, I never make it out of the cutting room. I didn't mean to kill the editor's wife. She attacked my secretaries and I was only defending them. I still get paid for my work, but now my digital existence has been reduced to a meaningless small-print credit. In my last scene, I met the leading man in a catacomb beneath the mall and we ad-libbed the entire take. He explained that he could play his character in multiple ways. I told him that the condition of my character was a matter of reaction, not action; hence my *becoming* was entirely dependent upon his *being*. When his entourage interrupted us, I liquidated them with an unreserved crowdstare. There was a beat during which the leading man imploded into the traumatic kernel of wet pulp that served as his engine; it hovered in the air for a moment, then fell to the asphalt and rolled away like a lopsided coin. Technically what I had done did not constitute plagiarism, but my subjectivity had been on indefinite probation since the last Guild strike, and the Studio's highest-paid admen were watching me. As I scaled a wall and took to the streets, I hurled makeshift bridges between the rooftops of the dilapidated brownstones that seemed to leer at me as if I might be their prodigal son. Skygods and chimneysweeps paced hesitantly across the bridges, wondering about the identity of this impossible stranger while recognizing that, *in medias res*, nobody knows who you are.

Buick. On a sunken dance floor, the camera revolves around the actor, who has fabricated a younger version of his optimum self, and whose shirtless hardwood torso has been affixed with drawers, each of which contains a shot of tequila. He recognizes us. Grinning a tall, ivory grin, he enunciates his line—a linguistic key that opens the drawers. We remove the shots, interlock arms, and toast to the Dead. The alcohol burns my throat. I discover my body in the trunk of a polished Buick. The vehicle swerves through a busy parking lot in reverse as the driver searches for a spot, dinging and swiping other vehicles in its path. I jimmy open the trunk and lunge at the driver through the sunroof as my arm falls into the weeds. This has happened before in different contexts. A street performer in a Godzilla suit retrieves the arm, and the camera zooms in so that viewers can scrutinize the physiognomic effects. The suit has been wetwired to the performer. When he makes a face, the exoskeletal reptile mirrors the intravenous human.

Dummy. The future is certain. Only history eludes us, dithering like a spoon in flames. This doesn't excuse the actions of the director, who led me to believe that the role was mine. The proverbial evil clown is the dominant antagonist, yet he only has two lines: "Billy is dead. What do I do now?" A killing spree ensues. It culminates in a northern lake where bodies bob in the red water like discarded gym equipment. I have been practicing different voices for at least three sleepless days as I roam the hallways of the Studio and graze on the constantly replenished supply of hors d'oeuvres available in the lounge. None of the voices work; they all sound pirated, uninspired, amateur. The director takes me aside. He reassures me that I have the part, but I need to audition again, and I need to use him as a crash-test dummy ... I lay him on the bed. I grip him by the throat. I forget my lines ... then remember and utter the lines in a thin hiss, adding: "I know who I am." Stirred, the director auditions and hires additional actors. "It is an interchangeable part," he clarifies. "Your identity is as good as gone."

Ennui. City planners have arranged celebrity graves on the road-side—not only to strike a pose, but to accentuate a point. As drivers speed away from Fostoria, they are immediately reminded of what they have left behind and where they are destined to go—not only in their vehicles, but in life. You can almost see the ghosts of the dead floating over the cracked earth. A free-standing sepulcher towers over the sea of tombstones. Above the iron doors is a sign with the words DONNY ENNUI etched into the oxidized stone. A lapsed Shakespearean, Ennui got lucky in Lost Vegas. He didn't win money. He convinced a mid-level producer that his presence would bring him good luck as he played poker. For hours, Ennui stood beside the table like a sentinel, blinking and breathing evenly, with elbows and knees locked into place, and by morning, the producer walked out of the Luxor $6.2m richer. Two months later, Ennui landed his first starring role in a gunkata film whose method director insisted that the actors use real bullets. His signature Heckler & Koch backfired in the climactic scene, which was filmed on the first day of shooting; the custom-made hollow-point bullet passed through his left eye, exploded like a grenade, and vaporized his head, shoulders, and most of his torso. The film was released as an "unfinished experimental short" and garnered excellent reviews. What remained of Ennui's body was laid to rest in this sepulcher, an egregious dedication to an unremarkable man that ensured his quiet reign over the history of personality.

Diegesis. In this avant-futuristic world, people live to be hundreds of years old. Overpopulation has rendered the surface of the earth an exoskeleton of Ballardian high-rises. Beneath the exoskeleton, an underworld of great urbanized stalactites stretches towards the earth's core. These formations occupy continents and oceans with the exception of polar regions where the New Irish Monarchy lives in stately pleasure domes. The crisis of longevity is a fluid hypercapitalist gambit facilitated by the Irish to keep as many "cows" alive as possible because "a live cow is a cow that can be milked." They began by treating all mass-produced food with anti-aging drugs, then rewired other *modes de vie* that average human beings would regard with apathy, if they regarded them at all. Enter a middle-aged Irishman who hates the idea of anybody disliking him. He falls in love with every large-breasted woman that crosses his path. One woman wounds him deeper than a berserk magpie. A cardboard-cutout love affair ensues, but it is interrupted by the world's indigent, indignant hordes, who revolt against their arctic superiors and threaten to ravage the earth from the inside-up. In the final tracking shot, the camera moves in on the Irishman as he stands on the lip of an evolved glacier overlooking an artificial lake. The sky cracks. Riddled by the cold, hard realities of experience, he stares at the horizon as if that glowing green line might be responsible for the Fate he no longer believes in ...

Colon. Bewildered, I schedule a ritual colonoscopy with Dr. Edmund Parkview, a disgraced Studio surgeon who was recommended to me by my dead father in a bad dream. A nurse wearing too much mascara helps me out of my clothes, removing everything slowly, one limb at a time. I chicken out when the anesthesiologist enters the room. "I'm still too young for this procedure," I announce. Arms folded, Dr. Parkview glares sternly at me from behind a glass partition. "Sir," whispers the anesthesiologist as I gather my belongings, "please don't do this. When patients balk, the doctor sublimates his disappointment onto the staff. It will feel good. I'll give you amyl nitrate before introducing the Propofol. You will like it. Please?" I apologize, put my clothes back on, slip out of the room ... and get lost. Nothing looks familiar. Garbage and detrital gore line the floorboards of every hallway. Nurses, security guards, switchboard operators, patients stare at me quizzically as I amble by, wondering if they know me from television, but oblivious to the überscreens that occupy every ceiling corner of the hospital, each of which documents my "escape" from a different angle ... The head nurse confronts me. She is a gross caricature, with a beaklike nose, pinpoint eyes, and strong, oversized hands. Taking me firmly by the arm, she reminds me that an operation has already taken place. I apparently "did psychotic things" when I was under the knife, and after I came to my senses, I showed no remorse, confirming her assessment of my "vast behavioral condition" ... They drive me to Detroit. I don't put up a fight. I even thank the paramedics when they drop me off in front of an exploded Radio Shack in Oakwood Heights. Stars blaze on the skyscreen. I lie on the sidewalk and observe the orchestra of light.

Breathing evenly, with the night weighing heavily on my stomach, I detect the signature of anger and sadness in every constellation that smiles at me, as if daring the dream to fight back.

SF. Pornography is exactly that which it pretends to be: a science fiction narrative in idle disguise. Dispense with genital aggression, people making funny faces, people making funny noises, and so on. What remains is an alternate world of fantasy with little tolerance for reality, not to mention the pornographic machine that has long been the engine of science fiction, arousing readers and viewers by exposing the metallic extremities and fiberoptic holes of technology ... Accelerating down I-90 towards Spokane in a convertible Lincoln Continental, I rev the machine as I pick up speed, pulling over only to buy more beer and solicit handjobs from hitchhikers, dogpoets, skinheads, and gas station attendants. I befriend an Egyptian dog at a truck stop and name him Aztec. As always, the alcohol takes over. I lose time. At least three days; possibly four. Vague memories of Spokane discotheques and old-school knife fights on fire escapes and rooftops rattle across the windswept expanse of my mindscape. Then I'm face-down in the hot sand. Dawn—the Pacific Ocean lapping at the beach—Aztec lapping at my cheeks ... I have an audition later this week for a porno flic. It isn't a major role. I'm reading for the cuckold. I memorized my lines long ago. I just need a cross-functional episode to ferry my dog and I back to the firestorm of certitude. Luckily, Terra Hipp shows up at the last minute in a beat-up Chevy Silverado. We make out for awhile in the cargo bed, desperately clutching the fabric of our pants, shirtsleeves, and collars. Aztec barks happily and runs in circles around the pickup truck. This crepuscular woman feels good and smells like Queen Anne's lace—not altogether fresh, and vaguely rank. Beat. At some point, Terra and I let each other go. I freeze for a moment and the world follows suit; nothing moves or breathes, not even the wind. Beat. Beat. Action. Panting and trembling, we collect our wits and adopt a viable line of flight. Scene.

Community. "Okay," says the director. "Everybody put on your Shitty Actor masks. I don't want one of you acting good in this goddamn scene. But I don't want you acting like you're acting bad. Okay?" The actors exchange glances. The director snaps: "Pretend you're in one of those goddamn *Star Wars* prequels. Act like that. Ready? Action!" Prequels? Nobody knows what he's talking about; everybody stands on their mark and hopes they won't be singled out. I am particularly bereft. I am an optometrist and must act according to the stereotype: a nice, pleasant, easygoing, intelligent-sounding man with a formidable lexicon who exhibits virtually imperceptible traits suggesting that he may or may not be a serial killer. How do I manifest my character in accordance with the directions? What are the directions? *Don't act good but don't act like you're acting bad*. Yes. I can do this. I always do this. It's my staple, my talent. Hardly anyone can walk the interstitial tightrope that lingers beneath my funambulistic feet. I don't even really have to try. Apropos. The best performances are not conjured, but already alive, dormant in the host body. All the host should have to do is open the floodgates, despite the director, who, stark-naked and hysterical, has resorted to shooting the actors again, indiscriminately, with no regard for the execution of our drama. Eternal recurrence—nothing can stop it. And I will only be singled out for a moment. Otherwise I am free. Otherwise I am not alone.

Benzos. Snorting a fourth line of Xanax, I pretend the bartender is not my father. How many milligrams had I ingested that afternoon? Possibly as many as thirty milligrams, but nobody in our circle has ever expired from overdosing on benzodiazopenes. The gathering in Fallingwater's hidden annex had gone on far too long. We were ordered to lip synch pop songs in a bedroom that accommodated more than forty listeners. I hadn't yet memorized the lyrics to David Bowie's "Oak Jaw," and when I heard Sam Struyk singing the song aloud, something the assistant director assured me was against policy, I stepped outside and absconded to a nearby hostel ... Feelings of guilt yank on my pull-strings; we don't want to disappoint the executive producers. Noticing my plight, my father turns from a patron to whom he has been passing off bootlegged one-liners. He tells me that benzodiazopenes are a ruse that exacerbate rather than placate anxiety while increasing the heart rate. "This can lead to bad valves," he assures me, "and bad valves lead to dead pigs, many of whom are smarter than humans. If only pigs could finagle the specter of language. If only the swine and the human weren't so similar. And yet we don't just harness their parts. We eat them. Mothers and fathers and children—we eat them up." I order a lager and begin to lip synch "Oak Jaw." Suddenly I remember it. The tap is slow and my father sings the song aloud, putting the lyrics in my mouth as beer trickles out of the spigot.

Ideology. After hours of intense scientific inquiry and assessment, it is finally proven that there is no afterlife. People who continue to believe in heaven and other forms of post-existence (roughly 82.3% of First World citizens) regardless of the proof are neurologically reconditioned to believe in reality (i.e., the certainty of nothingness, the termination of consciousness, etc.) by DmS (Demythologization Signals) broadcast via dumbphone. In the short term, the so-called "Reality Experiment" significantly alters the flows of society and culture. There is a period where nobody watches movies, television shows, or sporting events, the latter of which experience record lows in attendance. By Thursday, however, everybody has accepted the objective truth, grown tired of thinking about it, and/or increased their dosages of antidepressants. Media subscriptions return to normal, like life.

Veep. Even moviestardom doesn't always pay the rent. I book a side gig as the Vice President of the United States. This happens after the incumbent office-bearer dies in a run-of-the-mill Coachella riot and I discover a job posting for an ad hoc replacement. I deliver my inaugural speech to a bipartisan audience in Arizona. They stare at me like a giant insect that has pushed itself onto its hind legs, and I realize that I am underprepared for the job. I go to the library and check out the latest edition of *Vice Presidents for Dummies*. Between acting roles and political duties, I frantically read through the guidebook, highlighting important passages and taking fastidious notes. I bind the paperback cover in cordovan leather that matches my shoes and conceals the title of the book, which I pause to refer to during senate meetings, and which, depending upon who asks about it in Washington, I pass off as a ledger, diary, nutrition log, or bible. I recall one instance where I hold the facelifted *Vice Presidents for Dummies* over my head and shake it like a hambone as I proclaim to congress: "Notwithstanding the suggestiveness of their appellation, moth balls are not inherently anti-moth, although many moths have steered clear of their closet posturing. This is not a cause for concern. Rather, ladies and gentlemen, it is a matter of course." The book commands the attention of my colleagues throughout the entirety of my plea. When my arm becomes tired and I am forced to bring the plea to a sharp conclusion, I receive a rare modicum of applause. Things proceed in this gay, mild-mannered vein for months. As is customary, however, I take on too many acting projects, and they begin to interfere with my ability to lead. Bereft, I follow the footprints of my predecessor, buy a ticket to Coachella, and pray for the worst—which is always the best.

Reality. After hours of intense scientific inquiry and assessment, it is finally proven that reality exists. People who continue to believe in fantasy and other products of the imagination (roughly 12.4% of the Global Village) despite the proof are metaphysically reconditioned to experience the primacy of the Self (i.e., to fully embrace a solipsistic worldview and ideology) by DmS (Demolecularization Symptoms) broadcast via bionic implants. In the short term, the so-called "Reality Experiment" fails to significantly alter the flows of society and culture. There is a period where everybody continues to absorb pornography and patronize the schizoverse, trolling through the hallways, canals, and skyscapes of the latter with greater fluidity and dynamism. By 2059, however, everybody (i.e., 99.1% of the population) has snubbed reality, grown tired of thinking about it, and/or increased the frequency of their introjections. Dream subscriptions become normative phenomena, like death.

Incidentals. As I enter the ball room and survey the diners, I realize that there will never be another dusk. Everything is dawn now. "All of you only exist because I see you," I divulge, freeze-framing the diners as they lift food and coffee to their mouths, "and everything that you do has to do with me. My blasé nightmare is your exciting reality."

The scene unfreezes. An attractive blonde in a silver dress smiles at me as if she understands the traumatic acorns out of which my identity sprouted like an apocalyptic oak. I pace forward and unzip my pants. She stands, turns around, and pulls the dress above the dome of her muscled buttocks. There is no cunt; it has been consumed by the grooved, purple sinkhole of an anus. The moment I enter her, my vision falters, effervesces, fades—I know that the diegesis will rob me of an orgasm. Fading into ambiguity, I exit the ballroom and leave the building. Outside, the sewers have flooded the streets and frozen over. Several police officers have been encrusted beneath the gray ice in assorted poses of terror. I pretend not to see them, fearing that I am already down there with them, cold and rigid and stuck. Likewise do I ignore the vagrants that observe me from the red shadows. They know me. And they know what will happen if I miss a beat.

Home. Situated beyond the ninth circle of the inner city, Strychnine Heights takes its name from the genus of trees, shrubbery, and creepers that line the suburb's streets and crawl up the walls of its buildings. It's a beautiful place, small, quaint, and not far from the water on the other side of the valley. Catboats and schooners drift aimlessly in the teal inlets that reach into the mountains from the harbor. Cafés, wineries, boutiques, curiosity shops, bookstores, and fitness ateliers run up and down the steep windswept streets, and in the center of town, smartcars purr around an intricate stone monument. There are no traffic lights or signs. It is never nighttime. A small, pale sun looms beneath the cloud strata that seem to have been painted onto the desaturated, turquoise canvas of sky. Move in from LONG-DISTANCE AERIAL SHOT of Strychnine Heights to the nadir of Bodega Avenue. Bleach-bypass cinematography here. DUTCH ANGLE on the entrance to the Travelers Club, where the waitresses refuse tips and the vegetables are raw and fresh, like the rarefied air. Beat. Tilt upwards on the lattice of cellular windows above the entrance. The dull sunshine cancels out the interior light so that we can't see inside any of them ... except for one, a window near the roof behind which the thin, insectile silhouette of a man flickers like a black flame. Zoom in to EXTREME CLOSEUP. Hold ... Continue to hold. Do not go inside. Never go inside.

Lagoon. Every few days, the producers replace the director. They don't think he will do a good enough job and make them enough money, so at any given time, nobody really knows who the director might be. I assume that the current director is the operative director solely based on his bad looks and the resonance of his hoary baritone. He orders everybody to go to the hog lagoon where we will all drown ourselves to death. We have been shooting on the roof of the Dorian Tower all morning. None of us want to walk down forty flights of stairs—elevators were declared a blanket liability after Perrie Dune's dumbwaiter crash—but we do as we're told, with unreadable (or at least unthreatened) expressions stitched into our off-camera faces. Near the end of the scene, a crane removes my body from the water and delivers it to an ambulance. Paramedics revive me with an obsolete defibrillator and a shot of epinephrine. They turn me onto my stomach, make an incision in my shoulder, carefully remove a small fiberoptic mass, and encase the mass in a petri dish. I am forced out of the vehicle, then ordered by a new director to go back to the hog lagoon and drown myself again. I lose count after my eighth death and sixth director. That evening, everybody discusses their afterlives over sangrias and mojitos at San Chez.

Hog. Gene Pain wants to change his name to Barry Hog. Nobody likes the idea. The producers say it's a breach of contract. People know Gene Pain, but nobody knows Barry Hog. Disallowed, he goes on a two-week drinking binge in Singapore, not far from the location of his next shoot. On day 14, he tries to quit cold turkey and pours out all of the booze he has accumulated in his hotel room. The DTs assail him in the morning. He has to drink half a bottle of Listerine to stop shaking and sweating so that he can make it to the set looking halfway presentable, get into costume, get into character, and finagle a believable performance. The DTs return shortly after 10 a.m. Cameras rolling, he touches his earpiece and tells his assistant to make him a triple vodka martini. "Slightly dirty," he whispers. "Only one olive. Put it in a Starbucks cup." Fortunately, his character, Copernicus Gall, stands idly in the background of the mise-en-scène as two minor characters arm wrestle and exchange dialogue in the foreground. No deep focus; the lens can't detect the nuances of his skin, bones, and nerves. He clenches his fists, flexes the muscles in his arms and thighs, and tries not to tremble. A squib explodes on his neck region, spattering his jaw and cheeks with fire and blood. This is a motion-capture shoot. The pyrotechnician must have hid the squib there during makeup—another bad joke. Before Gene Pain can scream, however, the skyhandler yanks him by the wires, pulling him up the full length of the green screen to a veranda in the rafters. The cinematographer thinks it's part of the scene. And it might be. None of the crew bat an eye. Gesticulating uncontrollably, Gene Pain wriggles out of his chroma-key suit and lurches towards the nearest elevator, praying that his assistant has hit her mark, and per usual, wishing he were somebody else.

Intel. Last night the ghost of Donny Ennui visited Gene Pain in a dream. "I wish you were Barry Hog," said the ghost. "I know you," replied the actor. "I drove by your grave." The ghost made a face. "It's not a grave. It's a sepulcher. It rises above the dirt. Nobodies get buried in graves. Like you. When you die, they'll put you in the dirt. That's what people do." As he nurses an imperial stout with small, calculated sips, trying to detox by way of a slow beer-wean, Gene Pain remembers the dream, an uncommon occurrence: usually, the moment he awakes, he forgets what happened on the stages and screens of his neural theater. The contours of Donny Ennui's perfect physiognomy dangle in his line of vision like grapes on a vine—even postmortem, he envies the razorsharp jawline, the aquiline nose, the steel-gray eyes, the wingtip brow ... Refusing the comfort of a topical segue in favor of abrupt dislocation, the ghost continued: "Of all the wars that have been fought in human history, the greatest war—*is living with a woman*. I confess that men are far from perfect and mind their balls more than their brains. But the day-to-day grind of talking, touching, acting, reacting, telling lies not to hurt feelings, telling the truth not to hurt feelings, etc., etc.— the metaphorical bloodflow of a woman's permanent company far exceeds the bloodfow of all state-sanctioned wars combined." Gene Pain blinks and rattles his head, but he can't get rid of Donny Ennui's visage, which is becoming more and more pronounced, flushing with color and purpose ... He finishes the rest of the stout in three large gulps. The alcohol content is 12.2% and it will take the edge off. When the effects dissipate, his body will crave greater amounts. He'll have to drink his way through the day and restart the detox, pacing and sipping and sweating and quivering his way through tomorrow. "As a general rule of thumb," the ghost added, "you shouldn't shoot people who are running away from you. They pose no real threat, is the thing. Shoot a man in his face or don't shoot him at all. And if he's on the lam, let him go ..."

Sirius. The machine drags the lake outside of the Studio all day and night, pausing only when the moonlight shines angrily on the finger of trees that reaches into the water from the mainland. The moon is louder than the machine. Sirius Brain claims it has to do with history, with how the moon has always lived in the shadow of the sun. He should know: he has won awards for his work as a lightning technician. His last name is not really Brain, but his first name is Sirius, at least according to his mother, who is always with him, always monitoring his destiny, always annotating the differences between authentic and constructed signatures. The problem is that her nightmares about the moon's brutality are real. Genetic enemies lurk in the afterglow of evening as a bestial mania threads into the lunatic's hillbilly terrorism. I can only speak for myself. Sometimes the sun will intervene, not because of altruistic impulses, but in lieu of them. Nobody is as bored as the sun—in every practical sense, he perceives the moon as his arch-minion and effective doppelgänger. Of course, Sirius Brain's mother shoulders part of the blame; her last nightmare foregrounded a solar shuttle pandemic that scarred my hippocampus. Ultimately, all she wants is a friend to listen to her scatological revelations. She rifles through priests like husbands and makes her son into a holy malcontent. I often see him standing alone near the Studio gates. Gazing dumbly across the water at the machine, he teeters from side to side and struggles to remain erect.

Dystopia. A rooster wanders onto the set. Within the hour, we divide into factions. There are a few small, insignificant blocs that mainly consist of baristas, chefs, and production assistants. In the main, people identify themselves as "Pro-Chanticleer" (PC) or "Anti-Cock" (AC). The director sides with AC whereas both the leading lady and man take a PC stance. The Anti-Cocks joke about killing and cooking the rooster. This doesn't go over well; the Pro-Chanticleers threaten to call the Animal Protection League (APL), and it isn't long until the prop master does just that. When APL reps show up, however, the rooster is gone. "Either the bird left of its own volition," the boom operator cogitates, "or our enemies destroyed it." The reps inspect the set and conduct brief interviews with parties from each side. During an interview with the sound mixer (a PC with a keen interest in the vagaries of "fowl play"), he abruptly excuses himself and hurries away. The factions persist in the rooster's absence. Partisanship oscillates wildly. One moment the storyboard artist, videographer, and data wrangler identify themselves as PC, the next as AC, cajoled by the persuasive rhetoric of the AC figure-head, not the director, but an unassuming gaffer. Rumors circulate. There are too many to count. In the end, one rumor dominates the hoard: *The rooster was kidnapped by a neutral party from another set and delivered to an elaborate chicken farm where it now exists as the alpha male centerpiece in a groovy sex utopia*. The primacy of the rumor impacts the AC movement, which, in the aftermath of the director's and gaffers' pointed defection to PC, now consists of the set construction manager, costume designer, script supervisor, hair stylist, location scout, two stunt doubles, and three minor grips. The special effects coordinator tries to double-dip, making a case for the value of an AC/PC conjunction and her desire to cherry-pick ideological positions at her leisure. The director fires her. Shortly thereafter, the money runs out. Production shuts down and everybody goes home to drink themselves to sleep.

Motel. Humid today. The Hairy Florida precinct feels like Dubai in August. Even the iguanas are uncomfortable. What would Kierkegaard do? Doubt everything. Take joy in the strength of the absurd. No. That's Camus. Kierkegaard believed one must become a knight of faith. Like Abraham. Faith negates absurdism. And yet absurdism persists. No. That's Gogol. I exercise my celluloid nose. I can't breathe. The air is too thick, moist, and heavy. Even the AC fails to cool me off. What would McLuhan do? Apply jazz, upload an impossible lexicon, detach from the nightmare of reality ... I drive down the Strip sweating like a primate. The spires and pyramids and space-needles of the city skewer the ochre sky. I roll down my window and hoot at the living statues, the scarlet bards, the riot police, the work-shy banshees. There's a car chase. I lose my antagonists and end up at the Blue Swallow Inn. They advertise "100% Refrigerated Air" on a billboard that straddles the pink stucco walls. I get a room. The air isn't refrigerated. I call my agent and tell him to send somebody over. She never arrives. I prepare to shower. There's no hot water. I call the front desk. The clerk says, "Nothing works, sir." I call my agent and tell him to send over "no less than three substances, each of which is a unique type from a different family." I sit naked on the edge of the bed and sweat. Nobody delivers my substances. I get dressed. I check out. I can't breathe; my throat feels like it doesn't belong to me. As I manipulate my lymph nodes, an armadillo rips across the parking lot. It's on fire. A ball of screaming flames. Even its tail references the sun. I check in to another room, close my eyes, and pray for an angry moon. Even the sun needs to sleep. Then the darkness will fall and evaporate the humidity. Then everybody will be as unbound as Prometheus and me.

Exeunt. Michael Lassiter, Will Battle, Conrad Johnson, and David Happenstance show up seconds before they call me in. This isn't supposed to be a screen test. I haven't auditioned for a role in years. Are they assessing my reflexes? Trying to throw me off balance and gauge my reaction? I'll beat Lassiter, Battle, Johnson, and Happenstance easily, one by one, if it comes to it. But it shouldn't come to it. I go inside and size up the room. There are gray walls. No paintings; no photographs. There is a water cooler. There are six plainclothes occupants arranged in a semicircle around a camera on a tripod. All of them are strangers except the director, who I worked with on *Psychobilly*. That was early in my career, and I only had a few lines. (If memory serves, these lines earned me my SAG card). There are several free-standing lights. Nothing more. My flip-flops spank loudly against my heels as I stride across the room to the director and punch him in the face as hard as I can. His nose explodes like a squib. He tumbles backwards out of his chair and slams into a wall, puncturing the plasterboard with his elbow. For my last film, I put on 30 lbs. of lean muscle; I still don't know my own strength. It doesn't matter. "If you think I'm gonna read lines for you Morlocks," I announce to the director's colleagues, "you're dumber than you fuckin' look, you dumb-lookin' motherfuckers." Beat. "I'll kill every single one of you, goddamn it." Beat. "You think I'm some kinda fucking prole? I leave the shit-eating to the shit-eaters. Do you know who I am? Speak up!" The room clears. I help the director back into his chair, remove his sport jacket, crumple it into a ball, and plug his nose until the bleeding stops. "You fucked up," I say. "I don't know what you're trying to prove, but in the future, think before you act like a goddamn turd, you ugly sonofa-bitch." I punch him in the jaw and knock him out of the chair again. He yelps, gurgles, twitches, and faints. I check his pulse to see if he's alive, then leave.

Absentia. As we exit the building, Lassiter makes a snide comment about my flipflops. He's trying to provoke me. Like Battle, Johnson, and Happenstance, his flipflops are midlist Gucci knockoffs, whereas mine were handmade by a direct descendant of the Maharishi at a Transcendental Meditation retreat in Playa del Carmen. I don't engage him. He continues to niggle me. I put him in a headlock and choke him out. We smoke cigarettes and talk about celebrity jailbait until he wakes up, then get drunk on tequila and storm a minimum security rehab facility, roughhousing nurses, counselors, interventionists, social workers, therapists, and psychiatrists in a deranged fit. Meanwhile, my agent leaves a message informing me that I nailed the audition and clinched the lead in *The Autobiography of Donny Ennui*. As a result, Morton Leftbank backed out as executive producer and Barrymore Steed picked up the reigns. He wants me in Avignon by Tuesday for preproduction. I don't check my messages until Wednesday, so they give the role to Hank Burke, who dies in a car crash en route to the airport, joining the ranks of Grace Kelly, James Dean, Sam Kinison, Randy Savage, Albert Camus, Roland Barthes, Edwin de Bruns, Left-Eye, Roger Vienna, F.W. Murnau,

Jayne Mansfield, Princess Di, P. Woodward Still, Orion Oberon, and so many others. I lose time. A limo driver escorts me into the Hôtel La Mirande. "Booze, yes," I tell the concierge. "Bring all of the booze, *s'ill vous plaît*. No hard drugs. *La violence, la haine, et le mal sont mes seules drogues*." He doesn't understand my accent or my conjugation. I realize that I'm acting strange. I veer into the hotel restaurant, slip behind the bar, find a bottle of chilled Grand Marnier, and wander outside where painted stiltwalkers flow up and down the thin streets of the city center like Martian tripods. Pulling from the bottle, I remember that I've been here before, at this location, in this body, drinking this liquor … inhabiting this moment. Which has not yet happened. Which is, technically, "futuristic," even if the strippers in the windows are made of clay. There will be no upholstered apocalypse on my watch. As always, the diegesis comes into deep focus when I let down my guard, losing and finding myself over and over, all at once, and never again.

INTERBEING

Medias. A whale crashes on the outskirts of a forest that defines the northwestern contours of Strychnine Heights. It produces a minor earthquake on impact. Tons and tons of clotted leviathan gore erupt from incalculable orifices as the whale rolls across the grass, carving a ravine in its wake. The paddle fins twitch and flap like live-wires. The dorsal fin vacillates, erect one moment, flaccid the next, hammering the earth with the force of ten thousand sledgeham-mers. A great gray tongue reaches out of warped and ruined jaws. Carnage gushes from the spout-hole and anus and forms rivulets in the grass that merge into a single, raging watercourse. The beast moans like a cosmic poltergeist as its heart bursts. Then it falls onto its belly, sounds the final mantras of its death throes, and comes to a perfect rest as fumes hiss from tears and gashes in its demolished purple hide. Moments later, the dorsal fin curls into a fist.

2

Father. Ray Whirr was the first celebrity to sell his tears for a profit that earned the respect of his future detractors. Others had tried, but to little avail, and they certainly didn't make enough money to enjoy an extravagant lifestyle. The reason for Whirr's success remains a mystery. A jackripper cum gameshow host and movie star, he sealed ten individual tears in evaporation-proof bottles and auctioned them off at various estate sales in prominent beachfront neighborhoods. When one of the tears sold for 12k, he knew he was onto something. He began appearing at Comic-Cons across the nation. Sitting behind the counter of what looked like a 1950s LR (Late Reality) kissing booth, he could cry on a dime. He even encouraged fans to induce him by telling a sad story or calling him names; in this way, a tear might take on special meaning by forever being affixed to a buyer's personal interaction and history with the icon. Who cares if there was no real connection between the action and reaction, the cause and effect? Whirr became more of an attraction than the biggest comic-book superheroes and villains. At the height of his popularity, he commanded upwards of 200k per tear. The jaws of greed soon clamped down, however, and he started to sling other forms of non-scatological discharge on the side, such as lost calories, residual thoughts, and "baited breaths," offering the latter for sale on homemade fishhooks. Evicted, he returned to the gutter of cinema. He starred in four blockbuster movies before suffering a massive heart attack and falling dead on the set of *Behold the Man*, an adaptation of Michael Moorcock's 1969 LR novel in which he played an average Joe who accidentally becomes Jesus. Enough footage had been shot to complete the film. In light of the subject matter, a brief movement ensued, with fans expecting Whirr to return from the dead, and with his "bottled grief" fetching more than original Cézannes and Pollacks. Curiously, only his mother, sister, and personal assistant attended his funeral, where no tears were shed, but like Thomas Edison and Henry Ford, he is now recognized as the father of an industry that feeds on its own effortless momentum.

Fortress. Beat. Then: "In everybody's head, there is a voice that tells them that they will be the first person who will live forever and never die. In some people, this voice is loud and imperious; in others, it's meek and barely audible. The difference between my voice and your voice is that mine never lies. It always tells the truth. Hence my ontological precision." Beat. Then: "That said, it would be obtuse not to confess that we are involved in the business of lying. The human race, I mean. We are a civilization of liars and telltales. Obviously. We are only who we are because of the fictions we swaddle ourselves in. Without these fictions, we are no better than insects and reptiles." He chuckles awkwardly. "There is no gin in the drinking water. How could there be? Everybody would be drunk." Beat. "God, I love gin." He glares at me, as if insulted, then delivers a wide, white, spring-loaded grin. "Can you believe that sonofabitch won best actor? Fucker. These piece-of-shit award shows are all shit shows. I've been nominated over thirty times. Doesn't mean a damn thing. They don't even have any liquor behind the bar. Fucking hillbillies." He swallows the grin and turns to the wall. "Actors are superfluous anyway. The only thing keeping us alive is the Union. Once they kill all of the Marxists, we'll have to go back to being pre-agricultural foragers. Most of us won't survive this reversion to a society of technologically enhanced hunters and gatherers. The Techno-Spartans will evolve quickly, aided and abetted by better diets, leaner muscles, bionic implants, and supercharged imaginations. Then we can start to thin out the population before *Soylent Green* becomes the dominant unreality." Beat.

"In the end, the actors are gonna win. We will extinguish the rest of humanity, just like the Sapiens extinguished the Neanderthals, and we will build a new civilization, one composed exclusively of *artistes*. That's where I want to live. That's my Idaho, goddamn it." The urinal flushes. He walks to a sink, washes his hands, and stares at himself in the mirror, studying the chiaroscuro that the vanity lights cast onto the chiseled canvas of his face. I hold my breath and wait for him to go. I close my eyes and pray that nobody else enters the pissoir. In order to relieve myself, to exit myself, to annihilate and remake myself—I must be alone with myself.

Fraction. The walls have been arranged so that the dimensions of the room clash with my outfit. Losing patience, I summon the costume designer. She enters the hallway and proceeds towards me like a suspicious rodent, limbs twitching and eyes alert. I can feel her angst on a cellular level. My elbow comes loose. Part of my foot melts into the floorboards. The only agency is action—moving forward, never looking back. I fracture into a thousand representations of my primordial self, all of whom attack one another without taking sides. Nobody becomes allies; it is every lousy fraction-representation for himself. Meanwhile I have begun to massage the costume designer's smooth white thigh. I lose my fingers in her sharp knees, which erupt into a weird isometry of metric space. This is a nonconsensual scenario, but neither party knows who wants to play the victim. We may be screening the first victimless crime in human history, committed on behalf of vogue and metaphysics. It won't last long. Special offers rarely do. I whisper in her ear, "I have never been to Texas," as if confessing a murder. Contrary to popular belief, blood is not meant to spill on bone; they exist side-by-side in the human body, relying on one another for sustenance, for *life*, but blood and bone never actually touch in their natural habitat. Only under duress (e.g., a compound fracture, an amputation, etc.) do they make contact. The costume designer bites my lips as she kisses me and emits a midnight growl. On the primeval savannah, we make love beneath the jaguars. Dreams of Pangea empty into the showroom. It's sheer ideation. Memories of the supercontinent do not exist in my DNA. The most primitive human species didn't evolve until that coagulated landscape—like my corporeal referent and my ethereal signifier—had fractured into a thousand representations of itself. We can't access experiences that predate our ancestors. There is no cognition in stardust. Personally, I find it difficult to go back further than the aquatic apes. What I wouldn't give to occupy the skin of a tadpole, the polymer of a microbe.

Tomorrow. *Fade on.* "The only dreams that count are the ones that endorse the arrow of reality. Everything else is residua, detritus, ephemera, flotsam and jetsam. Last month, I dreamed I had perfect vision, and goddamn it if I can't see my bones through my pores at this very moment." *Pauses. Raises arm and gazes into skin.* "Hmm. Well, if those aren't my bones, perception is always as we want it to be." *Pauses. Sprays audience with gunfire.* "That never happened. Nothing ever happens until my pupils swallow your irises. Then the whites. Then the skull, the hairdo, and so on. This might be my greatest performance. I can't remember the last time I danced across the ceiling with the ghost of tomorrow." *Strikes a pose and reveals the ghost's cleavage to the amphitheater of exquisite corpses. Tosses ghost into the orchestra pit and strides offscreen. To the cinematographer:* "The scene is over when I say it's over!" *To the stage manager:* "The same goes for you." *To the leaves in the dirt:* "There is no such thing as original energy. All of my actions support this bald, bearded avowal."

Backshadow. In the early 70s, realtime cetologist Dr. Otto Dykstra pinpointed the year that whales would go extinct. He foretold the death of the last whale to within a week of its final, explosive exhalation. He even anticipated that it would be a suicide. Coincidentally, the decrease in the whale population mirrored the demise of tapeworms, which succumbed to extinction the same year, and which, for 76 hours, equaled whales in number. Popular futurologists hearkened back to that 76 hours more than scientific historians, arguing that it signified an as-of-yet unidentified correlation that would prove to be apocalyptic in the next century. Amateur detractors shrugged off the hypothesis. In their view, species have appeared, languished, disappeared, and reappeared on multiple occasions throughout geological history. Whales were not the first whales, they claimed, just as Pangea was not the first supercontinent. The earth's dirt has been clotting, unclotting, and reclotting for eons. A recent biopic about Dr. Dykstra's life and works, *Precambrian Otto*, capitalizes on this statistic even though it has little to do with what the cetologist achieved, how he behaved, and who he made love to. Nonetheless the documentary has generated Oscar buzz across the board, notably for best supporting actress (Natalie Wichita) and cinematography (Abner "The Human" Person). Moreover, as director Lee Simian has noted in many interviews, every aspect of humanity, including great migrations and world wars as much as bad breath and sidelong glances, can be meaningfully traced back to that which existed in our absence. "In absence is presence," Simian frequently remarks during publicity junkets.

Bos'n. A killing doesn't necessarily yield a killer. Consider hurricanes. Last year alone they wiped out upwards of 4% of the population. They are bona fide serial killers. Yet these torrential, terroristic storms are not sentient and don't mean to do it. Or not do it. Hurricanes are as friendly as they are evil; they possess no volition with which to harm a flea; the havoc they wreak is a sheer byproduct of their off-the-cuff existence. "Action!" Contemporary berserkers are insecure poseurs who perceive the world in black-and-white terms. Their aggression is easily deflected and put in check with just a few emasculating heckles at which point they retreat to the pub where they found the courage to act out in the first place. They lose their identities, then, and become docile bodies until the lifecycle repeats itself. "Bos'n! Bos'n, goddamnit!" The Irish in me (51%) dominates yet complements the American Indian (8%). My marginalized roots belong to the Cherokee. I get shitfaced from gargling Listerine. "Who killed the Boatswain? Resurrect him." I explain my history to another doctor. Blaming the marriage of my genetic code and postcapitalist acculturation, he prescribes a mild antipsychotic to calm my nerves and help me get drunk slower. It works in most cases with the exception of my aftershave, which, when I apply it to my cheeks in the slightest excess, functions in the same manner as three shots of tequila. "Here, master. What cheer?" Technical support dictates that narcissism effects a longer lifespan provided that the narcissist avoids substance abuse and obesity. Actors must be or become narcissists in order to effect long-lived careers. Ergo, in the not-too-distant future, actors will dominate the earth. At the end of the world, we will be the only ones left. "Good, speak to the mariners ... Line?" The Dream Factory that lingers on the cliff overlooking the Gold Coast is a bogus operation. They don't use the factory to produce a false sense of subjectivity, purpose, and selfhood in the collective (un)conscious; rather, it is an outpost for laundering funds from Amsterdam to Kaanapali. They are all domesticated Morlocks. The rest of us merely dance in the sand with the Eloi. Once again, the jack of reality trumps the spade of fiction. "Fall to't, yarely—" Psychorrhea is no excuse for pedantry. When the light catches the rumple of my wildcard gaze, we recall the meaning of godliness. It has nothing to do with being clean— chic degradation matters more than B-grade diegeses in the sky. The storm throws mud in our faces, clogging our sinuses and irritating our spleens. There is no escape from human nature beyond delusion, fantasy, image. Our carbon copies dictate fatality. Believe it. Faith can only be obtained via the power of the absurd. "Right ... Fall to't, yarely, or we run ourselves aground. Bestir, bestir." *Exuent*.

Now. Life exists in the present tense. Like a screenplay. Like literary criticism. Even when the past and the future come to bear, one must employ (or at least mind) the present tense. The auteur and the scholar belong to the same realm of wonder and pragmatism. This is a tragedy without romance or bloodshed—everything is always a still shot, a frozen frame, a Jurassic insect petrified in amber. The present confines us. The past and the future are sleights of hand, delusions we conjure to assure ourselves that time possesses shape, breadth, and meaning. Any attempt to inhabit history and futurity is a thoroughbred fiction. The only reality is Now. And Now is the real Kurtzian horror. What lies beyond the margins doesn't hold water.

Singularity. If this diegesis fails to succumb to entropy and deliquesces under the weight of its own digital exposé, everything and everyone will inevitably devolve into *me*. One of my names is Donny Ennui. One of my mononyms is Curd. Another mononym is Starke, but Starke barely exists, and I prefer Curd … My autographs are legion. I have never rehearsed being me. I don't believe in preparation. Rehearsals are for quotidians who lack the organic capacity to summon and catalyze their performances at will, on the spot, under any circumstances. This was taught to me by Dr. J.J. Pickle before he became a household name. I still keep him on retainer. Once a month, he charges me $300 per hour. I call him every Friday morning, and he listens to me rant and scream for 15 minutes. At the end, Dr. Pickle says the same thing: "To speak is to create. To create is to fail. To repeat is to live." Aside from hello, it is the only thing he says, and I always feel a sense of calm and peace with the universe before I fade to black, far more than when I rant and scream at colleagues, friends, family, strangers, and my reflection. Something about Dr. Pickle's invisible ear is special. Without articulating it, without even hinting at it, he consistently reminds me that I am no ordinary solipsist.

Chaos. According to Sun Tzü in *The Art of War*, "Appear weak when you are strong, and strong when you are weak." This maxim is countered in a remark made by Sam Peckinpah to Dustin Hoffman as they sipped iced vodka in a tent on the set of *Straw Dogs*: "Never appear weak. When you feel weak, get drunk, and stay drunk. That way, you'll always feel strong." Reginald McZed answered Peckinpah 100 years later in an alternate 2071 AD: "There is more strength in weakness than there is in nonsense." This is also a response to Kurt Vonnegut's satirical observation in *Breakfast of Champions* that nonsense inherently exudes strength. McZed does not have an interlocutor; he utters the words to himself, over and over, as he collects random footage in the schizoverse with Arriflex retinas. He has no idea what the footage will bear. It may amount to nothing. In this diegetic future, cinema is purely a matter of found objectification. By decree of the governing Atrocity Régime, all films must be made according to the basic principles of chaos theory. Conception and organization, plotting and strategizing, composing scripts and casting actors, drawing up a shooting plan or a business proforma—these exercises are illegal. Even preemptive cognition can be prosecuted if the long neuroimagistic arms of the law detect such activity. One must gather bits and pieces of raw, uncut life (real or simulated), then let the chips fall where they may down the line, hoping the pieces form a narrative that can be comprehended, if not enjoyed and appreciated, by the pathological viewership at large. It is a new and impugned Wild West. Filmmaking has evolved into a dangerous sport. There are almost as many directors as murderers on death row. As such, the profession continues to flourish, and people love them.

Hyde. I come back to myself. This happens far too often. In order to come back to myself, I must first escape myself, and whenever I'm on the lam, I'm out like a light. To complicate matters, I have a greater affinity with Dr. Jekyll when I'm on and out, with Mr. Hyde when I'm off and in. My monster, I'm told, is an inconspicuous, unaffected, soft-voiced, selfless *l'homme des foules* who treats people with respect, is a stellar listener, and never makes waves or steps on toes. My better, normative half, in contrast, is a furious ape who tramples anybody in his path and wants what he wants when he wants it. For instance, last month, Vitruvian Entertainment decided to make a movie about the whale that fell out of the sky and crashed in Strychnine Heights just a few miles from my loft. The news leaked prior to being conceived and disseminated, and I felt the hairs on my forearms come to attention like a primordial hoard. In under a week, I had attacked everybody that mattered, submitted formal apologies in all viable realities, reneged on my apologies, became a Cuban ex-patriate, patented my own brand of Tequila, apologized again, returned home, attacked everybody again, and finally paid off the casting director and board of executive producers, which, coupled with nimbly publicized bad behavior, is the only way to land a decent role. As the reality of becoming the "skywhale" set in, the hoard retreated, and with it, my senses, my perception, my consciousness ... Desire is the desire for desire, but Mr. Hyde doesn't comprehend this simple truth. Unlike Dr. Jekyll, he has no Ph.D. He only sees the goal and operates accordingly, conjuring a stiff beginning over the grave of every end.

Repeat. THESIS: Analysts predate analysands. PROBLEM: Analysts can't exist in the absence of analysands. THESIS (REVISED): There was a time when analysts functioned concurrently as analysts and analysands, analyzing themselves. NEGATION: If analysts co-existed with analysands (i.e., if they co-existed with themselves), they didn't predate them(selves). SPECULATION: One day, a group of analysts broke from the fold and stopped being analysts; they became sheer analysands, and as a precious minority, their value became so great that they could charge analysts terrific sums of money to analyze them. Soon enough, however, the tide turned, and the analysands grew in number and evolved into the majority party, effectively surrendering all fiscal power to the analysts, who, as the new precious minority, were now in a position to charge analysands terrific sums to analyze them. DENOUEMENT: My analyst, like all analysts, hides how damaged he is beneath a thin veneer of affability, compassion, and sensitivity. Little does he know that he's just a hair's breadth away from being a serial killer, if he isn't already. He doesn't lack self-awareness, but he has no aptitude for empathy, and he either believes himself to be unreadable, or he has no cognizance of his palpable readability. I can see it in the nodding split-screen of his eyes. CONCLUSION: To repeat is to live, but to perceive is to fly. VERDICT: Not suitable as a shooting script in its current form. RECOMMENDATION: Revise and polish, then rethink the history of cinema, narrative, selfhood, personality, godliness ...

Pain. The widow of Gene Pain is suing Barry Hog for calling her names in public. She claims that his aggression was "unfounded and specious." On Tuesday evening at 6:29 p.m., Hog confronted Connie Middleton in the lobby of the Fostoria Hotel in Strychnine Heights. "You got old knees," Hog is reported to have said, staring at her legs. "What?" replied Middleton. "Your knees," reiterated Hog. "They're old. They're bony and wrinkled and old-looking. Like you, you old-kneed bitch." The exchange was recorded by everybody in the vicinity. Now Hog is firing back, rebuffing the existence of the recordings even as they continue to circulate, and arguing that Middleton's knees are objectively old-looking—nobody in their right mind could deny this plain fact. Hence her claim that his aggression was "unfounded and specious" is technically untrue, as everybody can see. In addition, Pain isn't technically dead. Nor does he exist, in the past or in the future, among other things. Hog has filed a counterclaim. He asks to be compensated for legal fees, defamation, and emotional distress.

Doom. Travis Doom forgot to groom himself before the shoot. It's in his contract. He was supposed to have hired a personal stylist. That was the deal. In exchange, he secured free reign at the buffet tables on any set. Nobody's allowed to tell him what he can eat, how much or how little he can eat, when he can eat, or anything about eating. The contract includes language to this effect. It's even in his power to usurp the director's authority. Last week, Doom cut during the middle of a sex scene so that he could have a scone and stick it to his personal trainer and dietician, who he hated more than the director. All this freedom is contingent upon keeping his body hair in check at his own expense. His back hair—two dark, thick wings of fur that cover the better part of his lats—needs the most work, but so does the hair on his chest, which must be sheared and tailored so that it form-fits with his pectoral slopes. There had been a two-week hiatus during which he didn't groom himself at all. En route to the set, a shiver runs down Doom's spine. He's listening to Billy Idol on the radio of his vintage Porsche Spyder convertible, a remake of the car that ended James Dean's life, when he remembers that he forgot about his hair. He only listens to Billy Idol. Nobody else's music has ever seemed worthwhile to him, although he doesn't know the names of any of Idol's songs, and he would be hard pressed to identify a single lyric. It's not even Idol's voice. It has more to do with his idea of the late punk rocker than anything audibly tangible about him. What this idea might be escapes Doom, and so what really draws him to Billy Idol, he recognizes, is a deep, recalcitrant ambiguity, one that no other artform has ever instilled in him. He contemplates this ambiguity, acknowledging it as part and parcel of the Abyss. At the same time, he contemplates how to remove his back hair and stylize his chest hair between the present moment and the shoot (roughly 17 minutes). Doom comes from a long, proud line of multitaskers.

Enough. There is a man who has only seen five films in his entire adult life. He doesn't remember the titles or any details. As a child, he saw every animated Disney film. He remembers *all* of the titles and details. He is haunted by the wet, sad eyes of small animals. In college, he studied business, then dropped out and decided not to get a job. One day he is hired to direct a film. He doesn't know why. It is later revealed that a producer saw him and liked his shoes. "I have a good feeling about those shoes," noted the producer. To cast the film, the man walks downtown and asks strangers if they want to be in it. There are arguments on and off set. During one confrontation, the man quits and storms away. The next day he comes back. The film loses money at the box office, but it achieves cult status within a matter of weeks for the innovative ways in which it violates the rules of contemporary cinema and breaks down the cohesiveness of official culture, exposing its incoherencies and prejudices. The man is nominated for an Oscar. He wins. He refuses to accept the award, citing Brando, but he wears the shoes to the ceremony. In retrospect, many film historians agree that this is enough.

Happiness. I carry the artillery of my emotions in my mask. Nobody can identify which emotion has primacy or what the physiognomic conflation of emotions signifies. There are no referent feelings, no fish in the flat sea. My feelings are pure surface. This is not uncommon. Sentiment mimics time. The surface, like the present, is the only viable ontology.

Newspeak. Imagine a forgotten alcove in New Rome—elegant ivory buildings, their fluted walls covered from top to bottom with intricate matrices of bright green Strychnine. Concentrations of the deadly plant have no apparent rationale or pattern; knotted bursts and wild blankets congeal in random corners and flat spaces, sometimes engulfing entire windows, together forming a universally evil yet picturesque design, like paisley gone bad. Strychnine has a firm stranglehold on Town Hall. Shoots, tubers, and florets reach out of the Venetian streets, climb the building, and colonize the roof. Strychnine grows fast, particularly in the suburb that adopted its name, a climatic utopia for the plant's development and wellbeing. It originated as a tree. In this place, it evolved into a vine, a beautiful rhizome that behaves like Orwellian signage, assuring residents that everything is fine and good when death is all around us, accessible in an instant. Strychnine is as ubiquitous as hot, syndicated gossip. Everybody minds it, but nobody touches it.

Look. Sources contend that residents of the Heights have been eating strychnine *en masse*, plucking it from the exteriors of their homes and offices. This has never happened before on such a grand scale. As of 11 a.m., only three people have been reported dead. Rumors of madness, on the other hand, are rampant and include everything from blurred vision to carny ultraviolence. One man who has been identified as Horatio Stubb, for example, is currently scalping people. Look at him. He has clipped and tackled a businessman. He grips the businessman's tie like a noose, depresses a knee between his shoulderblades, yanks up his head, passes a blade across the skin of his brow, from temple to temple, then digs fingers beneath the skin and peels it backwards until the hairdo comes off. Shrieking, the victim loses consciousness as his skull gleams in the pale afternoon sun and blood pools across the bone. Police are currently searching for Stubb as he attacks somebody else, a grocery clerk this time, grabbing her by the collar and tugging her over the counter. Look at him ... Sources indicate that the surge of pathology can be attributed *not* to strychnine ingestion, but to emissions from the whale that fell out of the sky and crashed near the Heights last week. At least five times the size of a blue whale, the largest animal to have ever existed on Earth, this freak of nature, in addition to being optioned for an upcoming film, will be hollowed out and converted into a national museum. Look at it ...

First, or, "Memory" (Vol. 1). In my first memory, I appear in a dimly lit hallway. It is almost bedtime. I'm wearing one-piece pajamas and everybody I know has surrounded me—parents, grandparents, aunts, uncles, cousins—all of them huddled together, shoulder-to-shoulder, watching me, waiting for me to explain my anxiety. I tell them I'm afraid of dying in my sleep. "I don't want to die at all," I say. They smile, laugh, and rib each other. My parents tell me not to worry about it. "It'll be a long time before you die," says my mother. "You're too young to be thinking about death," says my father. The hallway carpet is olive green, like the appliances in the kitchen. My pajamas are yellow with white soles. I brush my teeth in a blue bathroom, then go to a pink bedroom and crawl into a sleeping bag on the floor. The memory ends here.

Mystery. There are no detectable toxins. Nonetheless one of the more dominant theories hypothesizes that toxins emitted by the dead skywhale have been altering the structure of individual and collective subjectivity. The structure of reality and the objective world hangs in the balance. Other theories are less astute and posit that the whole thing is a practical joke, that the whale had been launched from the mutant trebuchet of a rogue ocean liner, or that someone or something had fired it at the earth from outer space. The Vice President concludes that it's a magic trick; everybody currently subject to the image of the exploded whale, onscreen or *en réalité*, is the victim of a crude but clever and ongoing sleight of hand. Alternate-reality theories bring up the rear. Combustible teleportation. The after-effect of a multiversal "orgasm." Perhaps the whale slipped through a tear in the spacetime continuum like a fat waterdrop. The Catholic Church argues that the sky is the ocean, the ocean the sky, and the whale simply fell "upwards," its causal monitors temporarily mistaking reality for a dream. Theories replicate at supersonic speeds, groping for oblivion, and the more they attempt to rationalize the whale, the more they underline the mystery of the whale. Whatever the case, consumers rarely dwell on where it came from. They assume the guilty party is a usual suspect: extra-terrestrial aliens, Turks, God, Chance, or teenagers.

Ablation. Before the Cartoon liquidated the Real, the dictionary definition of "caricature" was the antithesis of its current index: "a picture, description, or imitation of a person or thing in which certain striking characteristics are *understated* in order to create a comic or grotesque effect." The revision emerged at some point in the early twenty-second century when a global census revealed that over 72%

of human beings had enhanced themselves via prosthetic technologies, ranging from simple implants and hybridization procedures to all-encompassing body palimpsests and reverse-bonsai renaissances. The census included Third World and low-income populations; in many cases, bushmen and itinerants were more technologized than celebrities and schizomancers. "Caricature" isn't the first term to be revised in the wake of sociocultural shifts (e.g., "ultraviolence" now means something closer to strong tea rather than impossibly excessive gore), but it has problematized the nature of experience and communication. Pathology and subjectivity have long been interchangeable terms. Now we must contend with never knowing if we know what we want, what we need, or what we mean after speaking our lines aloud. Moving forward, government-funded efforts are finally being made to immobilize our foremost collective desire and freeze meaning in time, now and forever.

Mother. In this part of the Heights, a street has shifted like a tectonic plate and wrapped itself around the base of Holy Mountain. The street used to be a haven for drugs and prostitution, but the city cleaned it up, and now it looks more like a stage set from an alternate century. Gravity doesn't work properly here; nothing falls where it should, and nobody gets disoriented ... The bar across the street from campus serves the best spirits in town. It's owned by a therapist who keeps an office on the second floor. She specializes in addiction, and she encourages all of her patients to drink in "relative excess" before their appointments so that they will be more inclined to speak openly. What constitutes "relative" depends upon a patient's physiology and the type of alcohol being consumed (e.g., the therapist sanctions exactly two shots of tequila for Conrad Johnson whereas I am permitted no less than four and no more than six shots) ... In the rearview mirror, I spot my mother weaving through the cars in the parking lot. She moves like a waterbug, geometric and fluid. The charcoal smudge of her hair belies her freshly ironed scrubs. I exit my Lincoln Continental and call her name. She looks over her shoulder and continues to move forward, yelling that she has an appointment. I yell back and remind her not to forget to drink her quota first. "I'm not drinking anymore!" she yells. "I quit!"

I yell: "That's ridiculous! Hold on!" "I'm going!" she persists. "I'm not waiting!" "Don't go! Wait! Wait!" She's too fast, though. And by the time I reach the entrance to the bar, the street has collapsed into another banal equation.

Radix. "A real god neither admits to being a real god nor pretends to be a false one." She opens the newscast with this one-liner and looks expectantly at her anchor for a response. "Uhm," the anchor says. She continues: "Likewise does a psychology of abstinence effectuate a blueprint for failure." Psychosis ensues.

Culture. Totemic statues of celebrities from real and fictional histories stand on almost every street corner in the Heights, as if to assure residents that nobody ever dies, even when they are never born. For this reason, few residents complain that so many tax dollars are funneled into granite, marble, bronze, and copper on an annual basis. Outside Curd's building, a statue of Ulysses S. Grant glares across the street at a statue of Mister Mxyzptlk, who glares back at him. It is an effigy of the deathbed Grant, with his cancerous throat rent open, smelted onto his crooked neck like a second, gory beard, whereas Mxyzptlk looks more like a lion than an imp, his etched, evil grin stretching into a cumulonimbus mane. For posterity as much as panopticism, a statue of Tony Grail glares down at both of them from a nearby roundabout. Ten times larger than the character he played in *The Cocktail Party*, Manfred Mann, Grail wears a longrifle suit and halo tie, a style considered to be the epitome of masculinity in the Whispering 20s. Such triangulations and blockings lend an appeal to the Heights beyond its deadly weed. They also bolster the tourist industry, siphoning visitors from downtown attractions that have fallen so far into antiquity, they no longer hold the promise of an imaginary future.

Guv. The people elect me as Governor. "I'm already the Vice President," I say. "Right?" My term begins immediately. Most of my first day in office is spent trying to tuck in my shirt; my pants keep spitting out the wrinkled tails; and the more energy and concentration I put into stuffing them into my waistband, the more the tails defy me. After a long lunch, I elude my cabinet, go outside, and take a nap in the grass. I awake feeling refreshed. The convention center disappears into the carpet of clouds overhead. There's a problem with the clouds; something about their texture implies betrayal. Everybody inside is celebrating the win with too much enthusiasm. I can hear their compensatory, over-accentuated huzzah. It sounds more like the racket that follows a loss. I rework my shirttails, fail to tuck them in again, and abandon them for good. Shadowed by a saxophone player, I go inside and give an impromptu speech about friendship—how it only counts when you're a child, how "real friends" are just people that don't badmouth or attack you on a regular basis, how "the concept of best friends" is among the greatest hoaxes perpetrated by mankind, etc. I think it's good material, but nobody laughs, even when the saxophonist makes fart noises and plays flutter-tongues from Late Reality surf music. This may or may not be a result of my disheveled attire. Afterwards I schmooze with campaigners and constituents as the saxophonist dramatizes my tone of voice, speech patterns, and word choices. A production of my rise to incumbency unfolds on a stage in the corner of the galleria. I'm in the performance and I have lines. I'm playing my campaign manager. Michael Lassiter has been cast in the role of myself. Enraged, I disavow my scenes when they come and go, spinning everything that is thrown at me like a cosmic turntable. All the while I continue to drink champagne and shake the hands of plastic women and masked men, who nervously assure me of their confidence in my ability to do good, noble things.

Ham. During a moment of social anxiety and emotional weakness precipitated by an accidental roofie, I invite everybody associated with the film to my loft for dinner. I haven't cleaned the place in months. I tell my agents and assistants to put all of the left-out clutter away and shellac the floors, and by the time my guests arrive, the vast interior of the loft stretches into the skyline like a hardwood beach ... A tall, partially embalmed honey ham rests on the long, marbled kitchen counter. I make a drunken toast and promise to serve the guests personally so long as I can get the carving knife sharp enough. "Please be patient. It may take awhile." I say this again and again as the night unfolds and I move from cabal to cabal, making smalltalk, and making no effort to plate food or sharpen a knife ... I find myself on a bamboo peninsula overlooking the water. The mirrored steeples of the city look uncanny from this vantage. Naomi Dare leers at me from the round bow of my arms. My finger is inside of her and there's lipstick on her front teeth. "Good feng shui in this room," I observe. "Look at how healthy and lucky that bamboo is." She tells me that she doesn't want to be my fuckbuddy. "I'm more than the sum of my roles," she snaps. I manipulate my finger until she starts to moan, then kiss the paperthin skin of her neck and shoulders. She smells and tastes like pork. As I proceed, I feel compelled to whisper into her ear about my inevitable demise.

Fidelity. The gruesomeness of the scene transcends comprehension. Even by cinematic standards. It doesn't bother me, but I can't deny a low-end visceral response. Blood and mucous and bile and oil form a crepuscular swamp that surrounds the largest portions of the corpse. Colorful, boulder-sized slabs of flesh—some smooth and glistening, others grooved and matted—litter the area like meteor fragments. Entire intestinal tapestries blanket the heaps of broken, pulverized bones. I step through the cavernous vomitorium of the whale's ribcage and witness impossible carnage, sinews, gristle, and nerve pools dangling from the ceiling like dripstones. I wander around the remake of the death scene for hours. Maybe all afternoon. I lose track of time. It doesn't matter. Research is worth the price of loss. To become the whale, I must excavate the simulacrum of the whale. It might be bigger than a baseball diamond. Including the outfield. And on its belly, it might rise six or seven stories into the air. Being here feels like reality more than a dream, which bodes poorly for the state of Yin and Yang. The real world is far less pure and far more artificial than the dream world. Simple oneirics. In the end, the unconscious always sets the terms of truth. Everything outside of the unconscious is just another exercise in artifice and subjectivity. The only difference between mammals and reptiles is body heat. Otherwise we are morbid equals.

Originality. I return to myself, wondering if the Studio will comp me for my ticket. It's not about the money. It's never about the money. It's always about the Principle. The museum charges far too much for the price of entry. During the investigation, flycams, spycams, and nanocams historicized the spectacle in tandem with actual film crews that used the spectacle for a wealth of fictional, nonfictional, and interstitial escapades. Reportage accomplished terminal identity and the investigation came to an abrupt, unsolved close. The whale was dismantled and hauled away, piece by piece, in a matter of days. Scavengers preserved and sold the body parts as alien artifacts to customers who resold them in virtual curiosity shops until media surrounding the anomaly died out. Initial plans to turn the whale into a museum fell flat as a result of a statewide political scandal about an altogether separate issue. Local authorities were quick to throw tax dollars at a remake based on forensic images of the death scene. Tourism spiked and caught the attention of the usual producers, who optioned the "preternatural resource" shortly thereafter. I have no way to tell if this looks like the original corpse. I have never seen the inside of a whale, be it real or unreal, futuristic or prehistoric, from the sea or from the sky. All of the clerks I speak to bet their lives on the authenticity of the scene. "Even the smell of blubber rings true," one of them assures me, testing the air with a finger.

Curd. "It's unique," I say. "It's oily, like ear wax. It's chemical, like glue. It's fishy, but not too fishy. There's something human about it. It smells like an armpit. It smells synthetic. I don't understand it. I don't like it." The clerk stares at me. He recognizes me. I say, "I think it's a prehistoric narwhale that slipped through a crack in time. Before narwhales evolved tusks, mind you. Animals used to be much larger. Megafauna, historians call them. Then humans came along and did what humans do: got mad and killed everything bigger than them. Napoleon complexes are much older than Napoleon. They're part of our DNA." I blink at the clerk and add, "This whale wasn't an alien. That's stupid. I'd sooner believe it was God's turd." I touch the wall. It's soft, wet, viscous. "Forget about it. Who cares where the thing came from? I don't waste my time thinking about it. It's not worth it. Same thing with death. You think about death too much, it's like playing with fire. You get burned by the goddamn truth." The clerk wants an autograph. How does he know I'm me? Nobody has ever seen through this public disguise. Beat. I don't like the clerk's hairline. Or his chin. Or his outfit. His nametag says CURD. I know a Curd. I say, "Is that your last name or your first name? That's a weird name. What is a *curd* anyway?" Beat. "I grew up in Galveston, Texas," replies the clerk. "Right there on the Gulf." Beat. "Oh?" I intone. He doesn't respond; he stares dumbly at my signature. Then, turning to a gristled pillar of bone, he drones, "The happy screams of whales woke me at sunrise, every morning, like the crow of roosters on a farm. My father was too lazy to get a job. We lived on the whales. We hunted 'em. We killed 'em. We ate 'em. Breakfast, lunch, and dinner, sometimes. They're mostly blubber, you know. It's a rich meat. Pure fat, really. Made me the man I am today." The clerk tasted the air. "I'll never eat it again."

Episteme. [*A tempestuous noise of thunder and lightning heard*.] Dick Frost stares at the camera and says: "Good evening. Why did you kill yourself?" [*Laughter*.] "I don't know," Curd replies, staring at his lap. "It was a whim. I don't drink or take drugs in excess. Life is okay. I work, eat, do things, get laid. I call my mom once a week. I'm happy, I guess. The only thing in my system when they found me were small traces of dyphenhydramine. I get insomnia." [*Applause*.] The camera pulls out to expose the palm of god's hand. Frost says: "I see. Why do you think you succeeded in killing yourself? This is curious. You have never been able to bring yourself to kill anything in your life, not even small animals or insects as a child. And yet you slit your throat and bled out with relative ease. How?" Curd chews his underlip. FTL opinion polls denote that viewers believe the facial gesture is more of an effort on the celebrity's part to appear pensive than a genuine effect of pensiveness. "I don't know," he says. "I think I was having a bad day. People have bad days. Right?" [*Booing*.] Frost: "So you were just trying to fit in, then? Forgive me. I want to understand. You killed yourself. You were pronounced dead. You were bagged and tagged and buried in a graveyard. It's all in the documentary. But you're still alive, is the thing." Curd:

"Am I?" [*Crickets.*] "Just kidding. Nobody should joke about life and death. I know what I am. That's all that matters." [*Exeunt.*]

Stability. Harry Florida Jr. sits alone in the green room trying to remember where he is and who will interview him. Two minutes ago, his people dropped him off and fled like hissed-at rodents. Something terrible must have happened last night. His memory escapes him. He relishes the loss. All loss is cause for celebration—especially when it's mnemonic. In the absence of memory, anxiety fades to black. Only when yesterday's images parade across our mind's screens, hailing the taxis of infinite dystopian futures, do we experience the Void. He becomes calm, so calm. Smiling and closing his eyes, he falls asleep on a loveseat ... and dreams about triangulation. His brother-in-law must return to London in order to make money for the family. Alabaster Seville met Lucy Florida on a skiing holiday in Alaska. They were married just two months later, securing a green card for the Englishman. This is the third time he's had to go home. Father went on another gambling spree in Durant and burned through everybody's savings accounts, stock options, and retirement funds. Sandy from the beach, he assures Harry that his confession denotes courage as they pace across the aviary's network of internal bridges. "Your sister will be fine," notes Harry Florida Sr. "So will Alabaster. By now, the English know how to do what they're told." I almost ask him if I should attempt to monetize my ability to fly, but I holster the impulse. Nobody likes a showoff. People like superhumans even less. I also can't stay in the air for more than 30 seconds at a time before gravity tames me. I continue to practice on a regular basis, swooping up and down the pier that reaches into the lake as day and night flicker on and off like strobe lights. People don't notice me out here, whether I'm high and dry or crashing and burning. I never improve. I never worsen. It's frustrating, but there's a comfort in stability. It's something Father has never known.

Finitude. As Boris Pachulski nears a wrap on his third *Dogpoet* film, *Dogpoet: Chapter 3* (out May 17), he continues to serve in the role of executive producer on an in-the-works *Dogpoet* TV show tentatively called *The Dogpoet*. The filmmaker informs *Nunchaku Weekly* that he and Gene Pain have a lot of ideas for more movies featuring Pain's titular bard(iche), assuming *Chapter 3* has a successful run at the box office. "I enjoy making these movies because they're complete nonsense," says Pachulski. "We have created an entire mythology from total shit. Plus, we have a studio that leaves us alone and supports all of our ridiculous decisions. If people want to pay for this and it turns a profit, I'm in. Gene and I could write an infinite number of sequels. Seriously. I could do this for the rest of my life. Infinity doesn't exist, of course—think about it—but you know what I mean. If people want more, there are worse ways I could spend my career. But, you know, we're in the entertainment business. We'll let the audience figure out the future." In *Dogpoet: Chapter 3*, Pain's character, Able Friend, finds himself at a crossroads following the events of the previous film, *Dogpoet: The Next Chapter.* "In the first part of the film, we basically just go back and forth between Friend killing people and writing in his mohair journal with a vintage ballpoint pen. There is no dialogue except for swearing and various unilateral taunts. The second act is a sex scene involving a love interest from the first film. The rest of it sees Friend try to come to terms with the problem he's in. I don't want to be too detailed and give it away." *Dogpoet: Chapter 3* costars Petra Raleigh, James Curry, Z. Delilah Prong, Bill Frank, Vincent Bison, Charlie Drakkar, and Hilda Pill Hance, among others.

Letter. I can't stop murdering people. I can't stop getting away with it either. I've also been getting away with stealing. Yesterday I filled a grocery cart with three cases of beer, six two-liters of gin, and whatever bulk-snacks I could find in the seasonal aisle, then calmly pushed the cart out of the store as cashiers, stockpeople, and security guards watched me go and did nothing. I don't understand why nobody will arrest me. My celebrity status would increase the socioeconomic value of my incarceration; putting me behind bars would generate seven figures in the short run alone. Strangely, I worry more about being labelled a thief than a killer. I haven't murdered anybody I love or know personally, but something tells me that this wheel of fortune will become an anvil of doom. Granted,

I did correspond with one of my victims in an epistolary capacity for several years before ending his life. I met him at a Comic-Con in Coeur d'Alene. He was a diehard fan of New Obscurantism, a genre that came and went quickly, but I had a major role in one of the definitive films, *Dish Water*, co-starring alongside Chanelle Wagner. In my last letter to him, I exhibited a rare outburst of emotion. "Dear Harlan," I wrote. "Hello! I never try to embody any of my characters based upon the way in which they are written. Every major character I have ever played has nothing to do with anybody else's vision but my own. I do the diametric opposite of everything the script says, if only to fuck with people, but for the most part, I feel like it's my duty to myself to create characters that have never existed before and that do things nobody expects. I enjoy disrupting the schema of cause and effect. All of my characters, in other words, are efforts to outdo and outperform the sum total of their collective identity, which grows larger with each installment. This, of course, means that every new character becomes more difficult to enact in a unique way. Honestly, I'm running out of inflections. You can only fool people for so long. Then you either have to die, disappear, or confess, none of which appeal to me. I'm frustrated. I'm lonely, too. Best, D."

Origami. Sometimes the Heights seems more like a ghost town than a flourishing locus of culture and the performing arts. This is primarily a result of the experimental museums and film schools, many of which have achieved top-tier rankings worldwide; when school isn't in session and the Studio executives decree holidays, life evaporates for days at a time. Long ago, the Heights served as the administrative district for the wider metropolis, but a crippling recession prompted a quasi-Marxist uprising that led to the deaths of legendary bureaucrats and the destruction of the district's post-Brutalist architecture. Certain "god-fearing atheists" were happy that, for once, Karl Marx's *Weltanschauung* had been enacted precisely in the way that it had been written, "proles" rising against and "neutralizing" their "bourgeois masters." As it turns out, far less of the affair had been "enacted precisely in the way that it had been written," and the aftermath didn't bring rain for anybody. The district languished for nearly a decade, demolished and abandoned, a chronic reminder that theory should always remain behind the locked doors of its own safehouse, leaving reality to the buzzards of quasi-functional imprecision. But when the plants and the trees suddenly began to push themselves out of the rubble, people took notice and acted accordingly, rebuilding the district as an ode to Byzantium. The vegetation accomplished a mass exodus from the rubble—in two days' time, everything was fully grown. And all of it was ripe with Strychnine, among the deadliest naturally occurring alkaloids on earth. The prospect of living happily among and within death's idle embrace appealed to a wide audience. Death, after all, had become increasingly alienated from daily experience the further humanity plunged into the future. Resurrection technology changed everything. Still, no matter how long one lives—nobody, as of yet, has lived forever. The collective consciousness reached a point where it believed that at least a preconscious awareness of and respect for death would ultimately build character and foster work ethics in the vein of Horatian philosophy. This contrasted with former versions of the collective consciousness, which felt that death, like everything "bad," was best disavowed. Ideologies of this nature led to the annihilation of what came to be known as Strychnine Heights, a Valhalla for the gleefully death-conscious and the bohemian-inclined, but only in theory. Practice was, and remains, another matter.

Refraction. Recent sightings by the paparazzi indicate that Donny Ennui is alive, but more than fifteen reality films confirm that he is still as dead as the sasquatch of Pullman Harbor. Like most of the Ballardian elite, he was an a-mortal being, outfitted with a bionic immune system, animated by millions of nano-robots that terminally built and re-built the inner architecture of his body, preserving it indefinitely from natural, cellular expiration. This did not exempt him from fatal trauma, however, and the bullet that took his life on the set of *Orgasm Sting Ray* has been reconfirmed by forensics scientists, who verified the body in the sepulcher where the actor was laid to rest. Ennui's needlessly long-winded will (i.e., invective) culminates in the stipulation that all of his assets be destroyed and includes the following coda: DO NOT RESSURECT ME, YOU DUMB MOTHERFUCKERS. Nonetheless, images of Ennui frequenting shopping malls, grocery stores, discotheques, and strip clubs continue to proliferate in the schizoverse. It may be a man in a mask. It is more likely a ghost made flesh. Who the ghost belongs to is what the media should be focusing on, not the absurdist impossibility of, say, a resurrection, or worse, a man who never died in the first place.

Agency. Without prompting, Barry Hog's team of agents multiply like locusts, and by Thursday, at least three of them have tried to extort him. He drinks half a bottle of tequila, takes the Concord to Florida, and confronts agent-in-chief Bianca Snyde at her Malibu estate. Martini poised in the lampstand of her hand, she's wearing a bikini that's too small for her age and grossly accentuates her medieval breast implants. Barry Hog mentions the "corporeal offense," citing specific details, then tells her she crossed the line when she authorized a coup against his "fiscal character." She accuses him of identity theft. He insists that he never stole anything in his life, not even as a boy, and they make love in the shallow end of a long, kidney-shaped pool. They fly back to California, making love on the plane and later in his house. For dinner, Barry Hog suggests they go to Zeytin's. They take the Tesla, and on Mullholland Drive, he kicks Bianca Snyde out of the car, slowing down to 25 mph so that she learns a good lesson but doesn't break any bones or damage her old tits. Two days later, the body of a low-level agent is found in a dumpster. The gamut had been run, and yet by the following Thursday, the extortion attempts begin anew, with double the cunning and aggression. There is no agency in education, Barry Hog reminds himself. If one wants something done, one must always do it oneself.

Synskin. Two American soldiers found a dragon in a Bulgarian cave near the Black Sea. It was fully grown but surprisingly tame, docile, and even friendly, like a giant beagle. In spite of enemy fire and probable death, the soldiers started to brainstorm ways to monetize the legendary creature of folklore. "We gotta get this thing onscreen," impelled one of them. "Think of how much we'll save on special effects. Synskin, too." Driven by purpose, the soldiers evaded the enemy and managed to smuggle the dragon back to the States, but they failed to account for the venomous knife of culture, and the dragon committed suicide within a week's time, immolating itself in a makeshift pool of fire. These were primitive times. Under a decade later, the price of synskin had dropped far beneath the gold standard.

Second, or, "Memory" (Vol. 1). In my first memory, I appear in a dimly lit basement. It is almost dinnertime. I'm wearing a diaper and my father is sitting by the fireplace in his olive-green chair reading a newspaper. The embers of the fire are louder than the flames. It must be winter. His legs are crossed and I crawl into them. I imagine that I am a hairy caterpillar threading through the branches of a fallen tree. I inch under the leaves of the newspaper and look up at my father. "I'm afraid of dying in my sleep," I tell him. "I don't want to die at all." He peers beneath his wire-rimmed glasses at me and says, "If god is for you, who can ever be against you?" The basement carpet is dark orange; the bricks in the wall are brown with black flakes. Everything goes together. The memory ends here.

Moby. In order to play the skywhale, I must first learn to be a whale ... I decide not to go whale-watching, or to study actual whales, or to read about actual whales, or to view documentaries about actual whales, or to learn anything about actual whales. My research consists of performing an enema on one source and one source only. Nothing else matters. The author has done all the work for me ... In Herman Melville's *Moby Dick*, a madman named Ahab seeks revenge on a whale that bites off his leg; in the end, he catches the whale, who drags Ahab underwater and drowns him. The rest of the novel includes extraneous data, flamboyant nuance, vast tangents, and pointed, purposeful symbolism, most of it conveyed via Ishmael, a perceptual vehicle whose character slowly dissolves into the backdrop as the story unfolds, rendering this first-person narrator little more than a Man with a Movie Camera. We never see his true face ... The White Whale symbolizes a cornucopia of material. Above all, perhaps, Nature (i.e., don't fuck with It). Also,

God (i.e., don't fuck with Him). And Death (its inevitability). And Life (the Horror, the Horror). The Unconscious. The Phallus. Ahab himself. Humanity. The Universe. The Unknowable. The Undead. Immortality. Good and evil. Happiness and terror. The absurdity of existence. Nothingness. The Aryan race. An alien race. The moon. Every crystal on every snowflake that has ever fallen onto the earth and into the sea ... Throw a dart and conjure a thesis: the Whale means everything. Ultimately what Moby Dick symbolizes, however, is a matter of subjectivity and that which Melville elects to reveal through the filter of Ishmael. "What the white whale was to Ahab, has been hinted," states the narrator, "what, at times, he was to me, as yet remains unsaid" (159) ... The most important puzzle piece of all is that I will not become a whale. Rather, I will become a simulacrum of an ethereal creature that looked like a whale but was clearly something else, something other, something *outré*. The rest of my story, then—like all good stories—will involve efforts to craft destiny from the bread crumbs of impossibility.

Kubrick. Stanley Kubrick's temper flares like a sun spot. Five minutes later, he has regained composure. He gathers the crew and calmly states: "There is a rumor going around that I shit on people from great heights. This never happens. If I shit on you, it's a proximate affair. You'll know it's me, goddamn it." This is the only behind-the-scenes tantrum caught on film from beginning to end. Together we screen it over and over, studying the vocal and physiognomic nuances. The first crew member to identify a subplot unfolding within the chiaroscuro of the director's face has been promised futurity.

Lynch. David Lynch never gets mad or loses his cool. He antagonizes you with passive-aggressive sleights of personality. We watch him politely reduce a hostess to tears before unbuttoning his collar and removing all of his clothes, even the scoop-neck tank top and striped boxer shorts. For a moment he stands there naked, shoulders slouched, black eyes held open by drawstrings, like a giant, hairless mole with a wild pompadour standing on its hind legs. The well-dressed occupants of the ballroom look at him expectantly from their tables. Only after the director puts on a rotisserie chicken suit does he snap into character. An egregious, self-referential nod to a scene from Eraserhead, the suit has been fabricated from real, cage-free chicken flesh, including the featherless skin. He slips his legs into the drumsticks and his arms into the wings. He requires an assistant to zip him up and strap on a mask. Cue music. The ballroom darkens and a spotlight falls on Lynch as he breaks into furious song, jittering his chin and belly, and tossing the microphone stick from wing to wing. Occasionally he strikes ungainly poses, enacts weird dance moves, and delivers crowdstares. He never clucks. The lighting is such that no subplots can be perceived or even extrapolated from the chiaroscuro of his face; lack of shadow makes it difficult to detect the contours of a beak, let alone a general expression; the scene could just as easily be a cartoon, but at no point does the texture of reality become a sacrificial lamb. Repeatedly we observe the footage in quiet confusion. My first impulse is to ask the director to clarify the purpose of the exercise. I wisely refrain. One never questions Nonsense.

Rigueur. Curd recognizes the newsman as Dale Rigueur. Dressed in blacksuit, he has the same off-kilter French accent as the character he played in *The Minister of Avignon.* "During my coverage of last year's Acacia Crisis in New Burma, I encountered mosquitoes with speaking voices, albeit primitive speaking voices," intones Rigueur. "But never have I encountered the likes of this. Recent footage reveals that the beast screamed all the way down." Rigueur's body dissolves into an electric blue sky that leaks out of the screen and devours the entire wall. Nothing happens, but then Curd hears something, a droning squeak, and he sees a dot, and the dot grows larger and larger, and the squeak crescendos into a galactic bellow, and finally the skywhale is upon him—Curd plunges into the hot, howling canyon of its mouth ... In whitesuit now, Dale Rigueur casually walks onscreen and jerks towards the camera, like James Bond before the overture and opening credits, only instead of firing a gun, he throws a harpoon. "Ladies and gentleman," he says, "this new footage has incited a tsunami of controversy and doubt. Previous footage revealed that the leviathan kept its mouth shut, so to speak, and yet here we see scandalous evidence to the contrary." Curd doesn't know what to think. Like everything, real and unreal, diegetic and nondiegetic, the new footage had been doctored for effect. Still, something about it seemed to be genuine. Rigueur adds: "Time and again, it has been suggested that the creature fell straight out of Herman Melville's forgotten novel *Moby Dick*, somehow penetrating the barrier that separates fiction from reality, whether or not the creature is, in fact, the White Whale. The novel went out of print centuries ago; like all literature, it died the same death as higher education. However, some reviewers of The Event argue that it is more than an isolated matter. On the contrary—it is a clear indication that the novel *is trying to get itself back into print*. The Event may be a deleted scene, they say, or simply a corrosive textual sublimate. Whether or not the text is sentient is anybody's guess. By 'text,' of course, I refer to a certain arrangement of words. In no way am I suggesting that every surviving copy of *Moby Dick* is alive and angry because it has ceased to exist in our cultural consciousness. It's not my fault that the act of reading became a practical joke. I'm Dale Rigueur."

"History" (Vol. 1). To whom it may concern: Hello! I have a case that has been in progress since the end of the last begotten century. It concerns jealousy over my heritage. I have been targeted by hundreds of people, above all Oprah Winfrey. My family was in the beauty and barber trades. They immigrated to the United States with Lew Wasserman, who was Ronald Reagan's agent. In short, Oprah and her entourage stalked me. It's no coincidence that her father Vernon is a successful barber in Nashville. They wanted to prove that I was nothing special and sent hundreds of people to replace me. Many of these people are cosmetologists. I will be homeless by February. In an ideal world, I would take away their licenses and publicize my intent to extirpate them so that they will never antagonize somebody like me again. This started more because of my family's political affiliations than their business aspirations. The case is really just an instance of reverse racism. They have even gotten involved with organized gang stalking in an attempt to kill me and hide the evidence of their crimes. I was denied everything. They kept sending people to chase me, paying people to abuse me, and insisting that I was wanted by the Law. I sent a letter to Governor Brown; he did nothing. When I contacted Kamala Harris, Senator Feinstein, and other legislators, the Screen Actors Guild decided to parody all of the rapes that they committed in the form of a terrific feminist movement. Let me be clear: *they are the ones who sent men to molest me*. This is a problem in the entertainment industry that goes beyond a simple murder rap. I will be dead soon. I am spending the time I have left to tell the story of how and why I was murdered, and who did it. As it stands, I still live where the county placed me, with two men who attack me frequently. Paul Marsack is a hairdresser who orchestrated stings against me. The other man is an indie SAG producer. Together they have used law enforcement to conceal all misconduct. Please take their licenses. They are both killers. They have committed numerous crimes against humanity, which include stolen property and totaling my car after an unauthorized joyride. Best, D.

Improv. Sanity resides between the thought and the action; insanity is the collision. Beat. Sirius Brain trips over a prop and falls into somebody else's dream. In it, a woman leaps onto the protagonist, who continues to stride down the hallway towards an ivy-strewn atrium. "You killed Jesus," she exhorts repeatedly. "You killed Jesus. You killed Jesus. You killed Jesus." Sirius Brain tries to shake her off. "Stop saying that!" The woman has ironed blonde hair and wears a disheveled kimono. The protagonist realizes that, if she's right, if he did kill Jesus, then he must now be Jesus himself. That's how it works. *What one kills is what one becomes*. Beat. The scene turns to salt and blows out an open window. Beat. Sirius Brain says: "I'm a script whore. I never veer from it." He tells the same thing to every screenwriter, every story editor, and every director. Then, within minutes, sometimes seconds, after the camera rolls, he begins to improvise dialogue, deviating into territory that has nothing to do with the action, character relations, or diegetic moment in time; he tries to make communication implausible and, if possible, inscrutable. First responders always react with malice. They deploy various intimidation tactics that the actor ignores and deflects, even when the director cuts the action, even when he locks down the camerapeople, sends home the crew, and suspends production. Nothing deters Sirius Brain. He continues to improvise like a jazz musician in a dark, empty, soundproof bodega, alone, for days and nights on end, until everybody wavers, caves, stops striking against him, and returns to work. Beat. In the latest iteration of this scenario, we watch Sirius Brain fall out of the dream and return to himself. There he is, docile, obedient, deferential, adaptable. A good man. An authentic, flesh-and-blood script whore. More than an ordinary metaphor.

Method. As the universe expands and flies apart from itself, my world constricts like a shined-on pupil. By degrees, reality and memory and identity zoom out and up and away. Left behind is the diegesis into which I deliquesce. I molt my skin and exhibit my organs. I shed my organs and finger my bones. The auditorium of my skull drops into the surf; a single-celled lightbulb hangs over the stage, flickering and fizzing with electricity. I dream about Èze—disembodied visions of the Côte d'Azur, medieval stonework, towering cliffs, colorful window boxes, exotic cacti ... DOWN-ANGLE SHOT from the mezzanine. A gasping minnow flops on the stage beneath the lightbulb. I watch it evolve and timelapse into Me, who weighs 800,000 tons, who breaks through the floorboards and plunges into the sky. I scream as I fall, and I never stop screaming, and I never look back. This is how it begins. This is how it will end. Illustrating my perspective, these lines of convergence will follow the rails into a central point as everything else—all of the sidebars, minutia, reveries, thought-chains, posturings, flippancies, and knee-jerk desires that make me who I am—pixilates and floats into the catwalks like the sparks of a bonfire.

Desire. I always wanted to live in Strychnine Heights. I dreamt about living there as a child. My parents made certain that I had traveled the globes at an early age, exposing me to multiple cultures on every continent, from the largest cities to the smallest one-horse towns, including a scientific research base in Antarctica and two moon resorts. Nothing stuck in my head like the Heights. It wasn't because I wanted to be an actor. Nor did it have to do with the sub-urb's proximity to Old Hollywood, an avant-fusion of Persian Gulf conurbations whose archipelagic construction had begun to evolve across the ocean of its own volition. The plant allured me—from a young age, I was abnormally self-aware and attuned to the flows of my death-drive—but there are numerous places in the world erected on, around, or above life-threatening natural and cultural antagonists. Above all, I was attracted to the Heights' weird history. The enigma of the skywhale had turned heads, raised eyebrows, and inspired cults, but it wasn't the first bizarre phenomenon in the vicinity. At the end of the 70s, a recurrent fire rainbow produced more mania than the fallen bogey. Formerly a "fire rainbow" had denoted a high-altitude optical formation that materialized when sunlight struck frozen ice crystals in cirrus clouds; in this case, a "regular" rainbow had actually burst aflame at a low altitude, so low that it scorched the roofs of buildings and burned some upper-level tenants to death. It came and went for almost a week—more than long enough to induce communal hysteria. That, too, had been called "The Event," just as every strange happening prior to the onset of the fire rainbow had been called "The Event." All of them were forgotten by the time the next spectacle came to pass—approximately once every two years. Strychnine Heights was a Bermuda Triangle, inherently dangerous, uncanny, and indefinable. Still, something else lured young Curd to the Heights, innerspatial pheromones that hooked his subconscious and wouldn't let him go. Maybe the unknowing was enough. One thing I did know: I would live here one day, and I would do something special before I died.

Turn. "I turn my body from the sun" (426).

Phase. I go through multiple phases every year. During one of them, I became obsessed with stick figures. There was no impetus, I recall, beyond observing genderless black humanoids on road signs; once, I watched an anthropomorphous insect slink across my windowsill in the moonlight. It began as a metaphor, my obsession—how stick figures are flat and featureless, lacking the nuances and details that make humans human, yet possessing two arms, two legs, a head, and a torso—all important (but not definitive) characteristics of "people." This was mankind, as I saw it, everybody I encountered an empty vessel, disinterested and uninteresting, fat and slow and meek, with little desire to do anything but allow things to be done to them. Days later, the metaphor begged to be a Real Boy. I forgot about mankind, or rather, I replaced mankind with myself, with my desire to become an actual stick figure, not just to "blend in," but to subvert and redefine the current state of the social matrix, introducing a kind of Zarathustrian wildcard into the formulary. It made perfect sense. I consulted my plastic surgeon and told him that a role called for the transformation. This actually might have been true; in major and minor roles, I have been in thousands of movies, and I am merely the base aggregate of all of my parts, most of which, at this point, have evaporated in my memory, leaving behind only vague traces and silhouettes of what I once became, not to mention that my surgeon, an artist of the highest caliber, has performed countless operations on me, making and unmaking my body and mind without missing so much as a gene. All I know for sure is what I want at any given moment.

Identity. "Rising with his utmost velocity from the furthest depths, the Sperm Whale thus booms his entire bulk into the pure element of air, and piling up a mountain of dazzling foam, shows his place to the distance of seven miles and more. In those moments, the torn, enraged waves he shakes off, seem his mane; in some cases, this breeching is his act of defiance" (415).

Action. "Leap up and lick the sky" (383).

Unbound. At the end of the last authentic century, it would have been an impossible feat for any actor, big or small, competent or incompetent, to play the skywhale without a dirigible-ready fatsuit and state-of-the art oneirics. The establishment of the schizoverse did something to audiences, unlocking the last vestiges of inhibition, and inspiring us to pursue our innermost desires in all walks of life. One of these desires includes the conveyance of "terminal reality" in cinema, notwithstanding the context, content, or genre of any given film. Otherworldly monsters are no longer rendered by puppetry, onesies, zoots, CGI, X/Z, N-1, motion-capture acrobatics, or any other magic tricks. Instead, they are grown on actors' bodies as exoskeletal polymerizations synched with the host's DNA. It is an expensive procedure that requires talent and finesse, but all major studios retain their own in-house scientists, who, considering the Great Disinterest and the collapse of academia, are happy just to find work and usually cost producers less than what they used to spend on makeup supplies and artists. Furthermore, actors don't have to endure the emotional and physical discomfort of preparing for shoots every morning for hours on end. The immense cost of synskin sufficiently voids all economic benefits. Desire dictates commerce, however, and studios have no choice but to pay top dollar for the promethean technologies that they unleashed on society and adjoined to culture.

Casting. "Bear in mind, Mr. Curd," explains Clytemnestra Bol, the casting director, "this role is *ohne Dialog*. There are no lines. We can outfit anybody in synskin. We want somebody who can *negotiate* this particular emulsion of synskin. Like fingerprints and retinas, all synskins are unique. Understand?" She looks at me like a roach on a stove. "You will only be onscreen for a moment. This moment is the key to everything. It will take months to shoot. This means you will inhabit the New Flesh for as much as a year." I open my mouth to say something. She raises a stiff, stern finger. "If your agent calls me again, I will have him killed. Ask around, if you don't believe me. There is no reason for me to speak with an agent. I take pride in never having spoken to an agent, not even when I was blowing my way up the ranks. If the fucker calls me again, he will be run over by a pig truck and thrown off of a cliff. Understand?" I don't have an agent, but I nod anyway. Clytemnestra Bol says, "You know the risks. To date, synskin has caused the early deaths of more than a few users. There is a good chance that it will destroy you, if not while you're pickled in it, then after you're ungrown from it. Whales are beautiful creatures, but they are creatures nonetheless, as crude and fearsome as a nightmare in the closet. So, despite the general obscenity of the synskin *im Licht*, you will grieve its loss, craving it with an addict's fixation and ferocity. Once it's gone, your sense of self will probably never recover, and that will be the end of you. You understand. All actors and artists are fundamentally suicidal, of course. I trust your affairs will be in order long before pre-production." She eyeballs me, daring me to respond, and when she leaves the room, I turn to the board of assistant casting directors and remind them: "It's Curd. Just Curd."

Subtext. "This velvet paw but conceals a remorseless fang" (372).

Gilgamesh. "We account the whale immortal in his species, however perishable in his individuality. He swam the seas before the continents broke water; he once swam over the site of the Tuileries, and Windsor Castle, and the Kremlin. In Noah's flood he despised Noah's Ark; and if ever the world is to be again flooded, like the Netherlands, to kill off its rats, then the eternal whale will still survive, and rearing upon the top-most crest of the equatorial flood, spout his frothed defiance to the skies" (354).

Fadeout. "The moot point is, whether Leviathan can long endure so wide a chase, and so remorseless a havoc; whether he must not at last be exterminated from the waters, and the last whale, like the last man, smoke his last pipe, and then himself evaporate in the final puff" (352).

Recycle, or, "History" (Vol. 2). To whom it may concern: Hello! Law enforcement will not prosecute Oprah or her father Vernon for what they did to me. I'm still going to die because of their abuse. It was put into motion by the Studio and the men in charge have never apologized. FYI. I am writing again in regards to organized gang stalking, which was arranged in Chicago and continues through the Screen Actors Guild, Film LA (since they work with government agencies), and the contract services division of the LAPD. The case started in Strychnine Heights, California, when Chief Lee Blanc was head of the sheriff's division of the LA County Board of Supervisors office. The whole set-up originated in Anais Watterson's headquarters and was executed by way of O'Melveny & Meijer's law offices. I have asked for restitution, but they are still hiding the evidence and lying about it. I called the DNC and the judiciary committee about Barton Heck's nomination since the people that attacked me in La Canada Flintridge and Altadena were from Yale and Kansas. They say my life doesn't matter and they already got away with it all. I have called and written every agency, the FBI, the LAPD, every senator, the DOJ, the White House, and Attorney Generals in every state. My efforts have gotten me nowhere. This isn't fair. The LAPD is still trying to prostitute me and make me homeless. They relegated me to low-paying jobs and minorities of every kind were laughing about it; so was the DNC and all of the other agencies in LA and Lost Vegas, too. My enemies have refused to write me back; in effect, I'm trapped like a ghost in the machine, with no haunting powers at all—I couldn't scare so much as an insect even if I tried. What shocks me more than anything is that *they did this for fun*. I request your kind response. Best, D.

Narration. "Since I have undertaken to manhandle this Leviathan, it behooves me to approve myself omnisciently exhaustive in the enterprise; not overlooking the minutest seminal germs of his blood, and spinning him out to the uttermost coil of his bowels" (349).

Quite. "Do you know, gentlemen, that the digestive organs of the whale are so inscrutably constructed by Divine Providence, that it is quite impossible for him to completely digest even a man's arm? And he knows it too. So that what you take for the White Whale's malice is only his awkwardness. For he never means to swallow a single limb; he only thinks to terrify by feints" (339).

Psychogenia. "There is no folly of the beasts of the earth which is not infinitely outdone by the madness of men" (300).

Third, or, "Memory" (Vol. 1). In my first memory, I appear on a dimly lit stage. It is almost showtime. I'm naked, translucent, with multi-colored organs, and my hands are grossly out of proportion with my frail fiberoptic arms. I'm sitting on a wooden crate—the only object on the otherwise empty stage. The crate has a rough top with dull splinters that prick my genitals and buttocks. I'm having difficulty staying conscious; I struggle to keep my skull aligned with my vertebrae. I feel as if I haven't slept in days. I might pass out at any moment, but my eyes remain open, alert, clear ... Everybody has purchased front-row tickets—parents, grandparents, aunts, uncles, cousins ... Only my mother looks at me. The rest of the family inspects the yellow program leaflets, carefully tracing the text with their fingers. Mother wears her third bridal gown, a minimalist ensemble with a beige skirt that, in her current sitting position, exposes both of her scarred knees. The vocabulary of her painted face belongs to a corpse, even when I forget my first line, "I'm afraid of dying in my sleep," and the prompter must whisper it to me from offstage. The memory ends here.

Face. "Dissect him how I may, then, I but go skin deep; I know him not, and never will. But if I know not even the tail of this whale, how understand his head? Much more, how comprehend his face, when face he has none? Thou shalt see my back parts, my tail, he seems to say, but my face shall not be seen. But I cannot completely make out his back part; and hint what he will about his face, I say again he has no face" (296).

Spine. "I believe that much of a man's character will be found betokened in his backbone. I would rather feel your spine than your skull, whoever you are. A thin joist of a spine never yet upheld a full and noble soul. I rejoice in my spine, as in the firm audacious staff of that flag which I fling half out to the world" (276).

Sirius. "It is plain, then, that phrenologically the head of this Leviathan, in the creature's living intact state, is an entire delusion. As for his true brain, you can then see no indications of it, nor feel any. The whale, like all things that are mighty, wears a false brow to the common world" (275).

Cervix. Gary the Cervix has been my wingman, handler, wrangler, and bodyguard for most of my career, since I starred in my first feature film, *Bad Men and Bag Ladies*. He looks subhuman, like an extinct species, anthropomorphous yet animalistic, conceivably alien, with a forehead like a dented smokestack, as if part of his frontal lobe has burst asunder. He frightens everybody that lays eyes on him. Like an aged couple, we talk about the weather, our medications, and what's wrong with who's running the world. When I have too much to drink or take too many drugs, he deflects attention from me—picking fights, stealing merchandise, destroying restaurants and bars, blowing up cars, starting race riots—whatever he needs to do to keep me on the straight and narrow. I don't know his last name. Nobody knows why they call him the Cervix. In essence, he is a practical ghost.

Scherzo. Curd always memorizes lines with the same music playing in the background: the Suicide Scherzo from Stanley Kubrick's *A Clockwork Orange*. The role doesn't matter; he could be a villain, a hero, an antihero, or an everyman. The genre of the script doesn't matter; it could be anything from a romantic comedy to a praetorian musical to an old-fashioned feelie. Whatever the case— always the Suicide Scherzo, over and over and over ... Repetition, as we know, galvanizes every actor, every performance, every effort to simulate the real world in both certain and uncertain terms. Without it, there is nothing, not even the exhaust fumes of "reality," which relies on the compass of repetition more than fakery. The scherzo is an electronic version of an excerpt from the second movement of Beethoven's Ninth Symphony composed on a synthesizer. Kubrick deploys it in a climactic scene that Curd used to watch incessantly as a child, marveling at the prospect (and proximity) of death as much as the director's cinematic gallantry and expertise. The protagonist of the film, Alexander DeLarge, associates Beethoven's music with violence and has undergone aversion therapy, reconditioned to become deathly ill in the advent or event of violence; even the idea of hurting somebody cripples him. In the scene, Alex has been captured by a writer whose wife he raped and killed prior to being neutered by the State. The writer and his friends lock the sadistic teenager in an upstairs bedroom. To torture him, they blast the Scherzo through the ceiling from a billiard room downstairs. Alex screams for the music to be turned off, retching in agony, clutching his ears, banging his head against the floor. Finally he succumbs. In voice-over, he says: "Suddenly I viddied what I had to do, and what I had wanted to do. And that was to do myself in. To snuff it. To blast off forever out of this wicked, cruel world. One moment of pain, perhaps, and then sleep ... forever and ever and ever." An up-angle camera watches him from the ground as he opens a window and leaps into the sky. Then we cut to Alex's POV, follow him down, and fade to black, just as the Scherzo ends, synthesized bells echoing in the darkness. For Curd, the scene works on multiple levels, including loose-leafed introjection, death-instinct jouissance, and prodigal revision, all of which he channels into the memorization process. Beethoven, Alex, *A Clockwork Orange*, the entire canon of Stanley Kubrick, everything that influenced Kubrick, the movie industry itself, the universe, The End—it all becomes a part of the characters he plays without bias to persona, desire, behavior, or personal history. He has explained this dynamic in several interviews. One was conducted by Kalypso "Ipso" Shadrach on *The Red Sky at Morning Show*, who pumped him on the subject for nearly an hour. Beyond the notion that all characters possess variable measures of good and evil, Curd never reveals the bottom nature of his relationship to the Scherzo. People generally think he's full of shit, pathologically affected, or doesn't know himself. The fact of the matter is that Curd is none of these things and all of them at once.

Makeup. Dreams make straight lines crooked, but they remain subject to the rules of social and cultural construction that produce and confine the dreamer, even as they appear to break those rules. When I fly, I can never stay in the air long enough, and it's impossible to murder people. Sex never reaches consummation; my shapeshifting partners always escape me in the end, changing the scene by force of inertia. Curiously, the Dance of Goats never fails to proceed in a way that suggests one of two things: inborn talent or tireless rehearsal. Perhaps both. As we have learned from countless runaway scherzos, suspicion and truth are interchangeable parts; if a man is accused of something, anything, he is probably guilty, if not actually, then metaphorically, or psychologically, or emotionally, or mnemonically—when all else fails, any accusation can be validated if we reduce it to the quantum level—go deep enough and you end up burnt by the telltale magma every time. Have you ever danced with a goat? They maneuver their limbs like dogpoets on ketamine. Some of them can perform complex moves, although I have never seen a goat do the foxtrot or the worm. A lot of dreamers think differently. Consider Travis Doom, who insists that goats can't dance, let alone stylize their movements and strike imaginative poses. This makes sense. Everything is a collision, an accident. And everybody's an expert—except the experts themselves. In other words, I am as perfidious as the next organism that imparts yet another subjective fact to the objective world, affiliating it with the audience. We are all narcissists, all egoists and solipsists; the only way to view the world (and your identity vis-à-vis the world) is through your own POV. It's nothing personal. It's altogether rational, realistic, absolute, and finite. Admittedly, the myth of objectivity complements the vacant cul-de-sac of empathy, but the latter is not a narrative. Remember: we can only see reality's contours through the lens of made-up stories.

Arboreality. "Out of the trunk, the branches grow; out of them, the twigs. So, in productive subjects, grow the chapters" (234).

Elusion. "The great Leviathan is that one creature in the world which must remain unpainted to the last. True, one portrait may hit the mark much nearer than another, but none can hit it with any very considerable degree of exactness. So there is no earthly way of finding out precisely what the whale really looks like" (218).

Joker. "There are certain queer times and occasions in this strange mixed affair we call life when a man takes this whole universe for a vast practical joke, though the wit thereof he but dimly discerns, and more than suspects that the joke is at nobody's expense but his own" (188).

Research. I have read *Moby Dick* 500 times. I need to double down on my efforts. Amplifying the practice of his posthumously adopted father, who read scripts 100 times during pre-production, Anthony Hopkins Alt. read them 1,000 times before he settled into a character. Hopkins Alt. once confessed that he "entered the dragon of the treatment" around the 750th inspection, but he kept going "for posterity's sake" as well as an OCD-fueled obsession "to achieve ten 100s, a quantity of integers as powerful as they are good-looking." Melville's epic isn't the script for *Ambergris*. It has nothing to do with the movie, but it has become my muse. The skywhale is not the White Whale, but my artistic liberty trumps the fictions of the novel, the screenplay, and reality, all of which I intend to conjoin, then season with the herbs of my imagination. I don't have any lines, but it's much harder to be silent than to speak and deliver a compelling presence. I will be in synskin, which, to some degree, speaks for itself, especially given the physical vastness of what I must become, but it will still be my body, my flesh and blood and bone and blubber, and it's my responsibility to fully manifest my idea of what that body should be, how it should behave, and the ways it should react, even if my task is simply to fall out of the sky, screaming like a meteoric Cthulhu. I have only transcribed the novel once. I can't decide if I should do it again or just underline and memorize poignant passages that will inform my characterization. I might memorize the entire novel. This variety of method acting won't really benefit me, and I'm conflicted about the practice. In preparation for his role as Nathanial Poe a.k.a. Hawkeye in *Last of the Mohicans*, Daniel-Day Lewis tracked, killed, and skinned over thirty moose, deer, and mountain lions; for Bill the Butcher in *Gangs of New York*, he tried to murder Leonardo DiCaprio on three separate occasions in private life. For *Serial Lovers*, Victor Bleep and August Eggman both actually murdered fellow actors, but only after their scenes had been shot, and whereas the killers were prosecuted and incarcerated during the weeks-long resurrection process, their crime emblazoned their celebrity. Method acting is frowned upon by just about everyone in the business. Most actors either aren't good enough to get away with that kind of affectation, or they're too lazy and apathetic to pursue it. More commonly, they're fearful of being ridiculed by their colleagues, even when they're the stars of the show. In a perfect world, an actor embraces the technique loosely, staying near the character in his head yet remaining himself off-set. Technically synskin could be categorized as a form of pathological method acting wherein the actor goes to the ultimate extreme to revolutionize the body and identify with the character. For some reason, nobody badmouths synskin in this respect. Every actor who has ever regrown themselves to play anything—despite the role, despite bad acting, despite box office failure—glints in history like a polestar in a constellation.

Mankind. "... the subtle insanity of Ahab respecting Moby Dick" (177).

Stasis. "These marvels (like all marvels) are mere repetitions of the ages; so that for the millionth time we say amen with Solomon—Verily there is nothing new under the sun" (176).

Ubik. "One of the wild suggestings referred to, as at last coming to be linked with the White Whale in the minds of the superstitiously inclined, was the unearthly conceit that Moby Dick was ubiquitous; that he had actually been encountered in opposite latitudes at one and the same instant of time ... Moby Dick [is] not only ubiquitous, but immortal (for immortality is but ubiquity in time)" (154, 155).

Primacy. I am not a real actor. Nor am I a fictional whale. Like Melville, who was not a real author, I am a retroactive zeitgeist, a generational mood, as true to myself as a monomaniac sitting down to breakfast. All I see in these scrambled eggs is the primal yolk.

Masks. "All visible objects, man, are but as pasteboard masks. But in each event—in the living act, the undoubted deed—there, some unknown but still reasoning thing puts forth the mouldings of its features from behind the unreasoning mask. If man will strike, strike through the mask!" (140).

Payback. "I'd strike the sun if it insulted me" (140).

Prayer. "God keep me from ever completing anything. This whole book is but a draught—nay, but the draught of a draught" (125).

Macbeth. "… suspecting them for mere sounds, full of Leviathanism, but signifying nothing" (124).

Bullshit. "I am the architect, not the builder" (116).

Bartleby. "All men tragically great are made so through a certain morbidness … All mortal greatness is but disease" (74).

Utopia. "It is not down on any map; true places never are" (59).

Difference. "There is no quality in this world that is not what it is merely by contrast. Nothing exists in itself … Because no man can ever feel his own identity aright except his eyes be closed; as if darkness were indeed the proper element of our essence, the light be more congenial to our clayey part" (58).

Inland. "You cannot hide the soul" (55).

Binge. You can't tell me what to dream, even when you welcome me to the Machine … In one week, the mad cetologists will strap me into the Green Chair. I fly to Cabo and start slow, sipping cervezas at the hotel pool for 48 hours. Then I turn to liquor and devolve into a days-long binge on tequila and *putas*. I need detox by Day 6. The Cervix flies me back to the Heights and checks me into a Man Plus rehab facility. Flooded with vitamin cocktails, benzos, and an anti-nausea medication, it only takes my body four hours to negate the DTs and detox in full. Now my head is clear. Now I'm good to go—ready to die and elude resurrection at the end of the line.

It. Somebody hung a mask on the wall. It isn't decorative. It's almost featureless. It might as well be a hat. The ninth iteration of Donny Ennui stares intently at the mask. He's trying to communicate with it. He's telling it to make faces at him by force of will. He's lying on the bed next to Chester and Adeline Sprague, the old couple that runs the Chateau. He can't hear them breathing. They might be dead. At first, the mask doesn't respond to his distinctively male gaze. Then it springs to life; expressions of hatred and angst ripple across the porcelain. Donny Ennui shudders. All of his ligaments tighten like guitar strings. He doesn't know why he's afraid. This is what he wanted. The mask heeded his telepathy and did what it was told. He can't move now. And the mask won't stop. Old Man Sprague snorts awake. He rises from the bed and shuffles out of the room into the courtyard. This is Donny Ennui. His name is Gene Pain. Everybody calls him Sirius Brain. Cocktail waitresses call him Curd. He paces around listlessly and finds a modular bar. He tries to make a Manhattan, but there's no sweet vermouth. He tries to make an Old Fashioned, but there's no bitters or citrus rinds. There is only whiskey. He abandons the bar and ignores how the sun makes faces at him. Memories of uncompromising vigilantism that might belong to another character play in my neural theater. I see my parents. I see the beaches of Maui. This is what happens. Old age. I used to be a telepathic virtuoso. Now I'm just a widow in a mask. I shuffle back to the bedroom so I can pray for the corpse of my wife. It's on the bed. Mushrooms and clovers sprout onto the skin. The mask melts into the skull. It forgets to pray. Quietly it watches the flesh timelapse to the bone.

Stage. In the beginning is the Hypodermic Needle ... The superheroic euphoria that accompanies the shot barely rivals the skid marks of my ego, but the cocktail numbs me to the core while allowing me to move my limbs with complete autonomy. I begin to hallucinate and mutate. My skin melts into the mattress like flamethrown wax; my teeth fall out of my mouth onto my chin and neck cords. I lose all of my extremities. I can see my ribcage, my sinews, my evolving gore ... When I scream, I inflate like a zeppelin ... Time slows into a brief tableaux. We observe my organs dangling like ornaments from the rising temple of my broken bones. Blood exits the floodgates in amoebic globules that circulate through the Studio lab. My heart becomes a tumor. My lungs become impact craters. My marrow catches fire; I can smell it burning as it oozes into the wastepipes. There is no pain. Then there is only pain. B-movie administrators hold me down until I take a breath and hurl them into the ceiling. "Ahab is not a man," I bellow. "He is mankind. And mankind belongs to me." They shoot me with tranquilizer bazookas as I pound the floor with my prolapsed rectum. I think I kill somebody—a loud crunch incites louder commotion. It makes me want to kill some-body else—all of them, everybody, even plants and the dirt, and history, everything dead and living and not-yet-born. It's my right to eat the world and shit on the universe. And even Studio proles have decent resurrection policies ... On the shores of desire, a megaloma-niacal surf ebbs and flows onto the rocks ... until the rocks submerge and the shore evaporates, reterritorializing my domain. This is the first of seventeen stages. This takes six days and seven nights.

Flashback. Like an antidepressant, skynskin takes three months to become fully affective and fluidly pathological. Once it does, when you are not acting, you are always dreaming, remembering, oper-ating on a high-definition, hypnagogic bandwidth. There is no need to sleep: your body lingers in a state of rest even when it becomes hyperactive. There is little need to eat or move: synskin regularly exercises your musculature and intravenously feeds you, recycling and purifying the body's water supply while providing you with ample nutrients and vitamins from the synskin's well-stocked cel-lular pantry ... I am relaxing on the teal floor of a deep pool. Artificial sunlight skips down the ripples, swells, and currents in the water and lands on my skin. The sensation in my fins is remarkable, but I can't shake the ghost of my fingers and toes, even as my memories of yesterday are usurped by the amnesias of tomorrow ... Even-tually, inevitably, the contours of this mnemonic palimpsest bleed into reality and disappear. Truth, like morality, becomes a myth in violation of its objective stability, tangibility, and certifiable abso-lutism ... I don't forget my lines. I choose not to memorize them. On opening night, I regret my decision and begin to rifle through the script. It's too late. I play dumb. I play sick. In spite of my attempts to avoid the theater—no matter how fast I run or how successfully I conceal myself—I end up onstage, or backstage, or in the balcony, the green room, the box office, the lobby ... A spotlight follows me everywhere. Even when I bury myself, the light finds me. My mind wants to disappear, but my body needs to be seen and humiliated. Only after my parents arrive do I begin to feel at ease. I know they will hear and accept my lies without recourse. My mother takes me in her arms and swaddles me in wool as my father glances around the theater like a child visiting a big city for the first time. His innocence and lack of worldliness anger me. "I only have six goddamn lines," I tell him. "What's the big deal?" I notice the lead actress talking to the costume designer. I climb out of my mother's embrace and ask if she memorized her lines. "Are you joking?" replies the actress. "We've been doing dry runs all week." I skulk back to my parents, who have fallen down a flight of stairs. The sound of their cries and the sight of their crooked, broken limbs comforts me. I know what to do now. The power of choice no longer matters ... Backstage alchemists edit the fabric of reality as the play unfolds. They don't replace me. My body, my actions, and my dialogue are "ingested" by an unseen stage presence that abruptly turns malignant. As the actors collapse, the audience prolapses, sinking into the primordial ooze. All of this ad hoc gore reminds me of where I came from, who I am, and where I'm going ... The fin lies heavy on the acrylic seafloor.

INTERMEZZO

Sans. "Surely all of this is not without meaning" (20).

3

Ago. The weight of the future; the teeth marks of the past—I can't decide which one causes more harm. Memory traumatizes us more than foresight, or so it seems: both afflictions stem from the same areas of activity in the brain. "I never lie," I inform the herd. "My memory is the one that lies. I simply open and read the letters that my mnemonic postman delivers to me. It's not my fault if the letters are misleading. Memory is fallacious by default. That's why history is a fairytale. The best we can do is make educated guesses about what happened in that pileup of yesterdays. It's in everybody's best interests to revise the past as it unfolds from the present like tape from a stock ticker. Cut and doctor the tape just right, and there you have it: *happiness.*" The monologue lasts another four and a half minutes. I read it to the herd directly from the script, licking my fingertip before turning every page. I can't remember the last time I memorized my lines. Not that it matters. The period piece is set in an alternate diegesis where special-effects technologies plateaued and could not be made better. This inertia effected a reversion to medieval suspension-of-disbelief cognizance. The New Culture forced audiences to exercise their imaginations rather than have their entertainment served to them on a platter. In some cases, actors were completely redundant. All viewers needed was a blank screen. This state of (in)humanity didn't last long, of course. Lack of usage had limited the scope of the imagination so that it only "worked" for brief intervals before short-fusing like a cheap circuit.

The New Culture became the Vintage Culture, and everybody prayed that the gods of technology would evolve special effects beyond the Terminus that threatened to extinguish life as they knew it. The gods responded benevolently—they had no choice. And here I am again.

Agog. Whenever he gets sober, which can last anywhere from a few hours to eleven months (he has never maintained sobriety for more than a year), Curd becomes the epitome of mindfulness, loving-kindness, and *chi*, dispensing knowledge and goodwill with the same degree of clarity that he soaks it up. He feels connected with everybody and everything in the universe and the schizoverse: black holes, disgruntled neighbors, rogue pixels, useless quarks—nothing escapes his infinite circle of friends. Obsessive episodes abound in the pacific throes of sobriety. During one of these episodes, he spent hours every night in the Strychnine County Public Tomb reading documents about *Suscaella* a.k.a. "shadowfaxes." These whale-like creatures populated the skies in the later Paleozoic era. This was shortly before the rise of dinosaurs and the breakup of Pangea in the early Mesozoic era. Growing to the size of modern-day cities, shadowfaxes dominated the atmosphere, even in artic regions, casting a blanket of darkness onto the earth's surface that limited sunlight and ensured that land-dwelling animals never got a good look at the moon. They operated like hovercrafts, clovered with fins that spun like blower blades and propelled their great gray bodies. They hated the water and usually flew above the clouds, and they never landed on the earth. Dirt, rocks, vegetation, anything solid was a potent allergen. Aerial fossils reveal that shadowfaxes were cannibals, but they mated and spawned faster than they could eat themselves, and overpopulation led to their eventual demise as they slowly layered their gargantuan bodies to the exosphere and beyond. Newborn leviathans froze and floated into space, *en bloc*, like fecal ice cubes, the moment they exited the cloacae of their hermaphroditic parents. It isn't known for certain what finally led to the extinction of *Suscaella*. Dominant theories foreground a meteor, mass suicide, a new species of sky-going predator, and a sudden distaste for their own flesh. The most prevalent theory is that their fins devolved and could no longer keep them airborne. Once they stopped falling up, they all fell down.

Ogg. The board of trustees replaces four directors during early production. Each director trashes all of the footage shot by his or her predecessor. The title of the film continues to mutate until the board settles on *Ambergris*. The fifth director accidentally kills one of the board members in a bar brawl, commanding the respect and fear of the victim's colleagues. The first day Donovan Ogg walks onto the set, he gathers the crew and says: "Hello! Call me Doctor Reverend Donovan Ogg Esquire. The prefixes hold water—I have a Ph.D. in How to Fuck You Up If You Fuck with Me, I am an ordained goddamned minister, and I received my Doctor of Jurisprudence degree from the University of Reality. This will be a movie in fourteen acts that lasts eight hours—480 minutes—the full span of a working day—not a minute more, not a minute less. Fuck the machine! Questions?"

Revision. In fact, *Ambergris* would be six days and nights long—144 hours; 8,640 minutes—and hinge on the sleep-deprived hallucinations of viewers, who could only watch the film from beginning to end in hive-mind theaters that attend to all biological needs as they enjoy the picture, the special effects of which are wired to and rely upon the vicissitudes of a destablized collective unconscious. This doesn't offset the status quo. Nobody remembers when delirium was anything less than the epitome of high technology and, by extension, subjectivity.

Inferno. Cinema, like War, is Hell. And inaction, not action, is the fiery catalyst. Both soldiers and actors spend most of their time waiting to shoot. Hell is the anxious visualization of boundless imagined futures.

Drop. "You don't know who you are until you kill another human being," says Doctor Reverend Donovan Ogg Esquire. "Only after you take somebody's life can you begin to make sense of your own. It's just like they say in the movies. Watch." He shoots an assistant director in the head. The head explodes like a cantaloupe, spraying gore onto the face of another assistant director, who faints. "Right. Now I know who I am." Doctor Reverend Donovan Ogg Esquire strides to the aquarium and pounds on the glass. "Hey! Hey you! Is this fucker alive?" Everybody nods. "Look, fella. My muse makes more sense than your god. I want to be clear about that. Don't go using your thinkball too hard. I don't care how big they grew it. Do as you're told and keep your snorkel shut. It wouldn't hurt if you pretended to be happy, too. That's all I want from anybody: a docile body and a dumb smile. Who the fuck are you?" Loitering near my canine, which is more of a tusk, Gary the Cervix introduces himself. He's never smiled in his life. He tries to. "Dear lord," says the director. "Your parents did a number on you, it seems." He shoots Gary the Cervix point-blank in the chest. Blood, bone, and organs erupt from of his back in long anime tendrils that, freeze-framed, look like hideous wings. "Nobody resurrect him. Given the chance, he'd do me the same courtesy." He punches the aquarium. I blink. "Hey! Your name is Fish. I don't care what they used to call you. I don't care if you're a mammal either." He glares into my eye, then barks at the crew: "Get Fish in the air. I want him eating clouds before my afternoon nap." Four hours and six murders later, a squadron of helicopters drop me into an impact sea from a height of 40,000 feet. The consistency of the foamwater breaks my fall when I land in it, cradling me like a sponge. My vocal chords have been evolved and outfitted for maximum sound quality, and I scream all the way down, fearful for my life despite the precautions that have been taken to ensure my safety. We do eight drops before calling it a day. More of the same tomorrow. Dress rehearsals will last another month before they start shooting footage. I have already gone insane. It feels no different than melancholy, apathy, ennui, and the unspeakable flatness of everyday life.

FX. If history has taught us nothing else, it is that the Year of the Pig spawns more cults than any other timeframe. During the last cycle, a cult made famous by its star-quality affiliates (among them Sally Code, S. Tor Resartus, David Iain Smith, and Parker Banshee) vied against synskin—or rather, *sin* skin—calling it an "organic evil." The cult's argument stemmed from a Union complaint. Sin skin revolutionized the special effects industry and employed more scientists and bioengineers than it did FX artists, the latter of whom became redundant in under a decade. Technological purists accused sin skin of being too "natural," or at least retroactive, making what should be a simulacrum more real than real; this diegetic superrealism, in their eyes, was no better than a vaudeville puppet show, even if the puppets were, apropos, "human, all too human." It was entirely about money, though. And the money went to the House. It began with the first onscreen appearance of sin skin, Finnegan Wake's werewolf, a remarkable inaugural feat in that Wake could manually activate the wolf and change from human to beast at will by thinking about a sequence of basic images. This creature was far less believable than the accomplishments of bygone makeup artists, dating back to Dave Elsey's work on Benicio del Toro in *The Wolfman*. It didn't matter. Sin skin may have been manufactured in a lab, but it was biological and hence perceived as "real." This knowledge prompted audiences to sacrifice unrealism for the sake of enjoyment: they suspended their Belief, and the innovation—which, the cult argued, was technically a denovation—won over their hearts and minds like the maiden injection of a genetically predetermined addict. In Wake's proverbial wake, consumer demand never reset itself. Even movies distinguished by seamless virtual FX were derided and automatically associated with New Poverty Row. In some cases, they were banned before being made.

Addiction. There are two suborders of whales. One has teeth (*Odontoceti*); the other has baleen plates (*Mysteceti*). Both feed on krill, and all whales are always hungry, spending most of their time on the hunt for food. This has nothing to do with me ... Synskyn feeds itself, but I still experience hunger for extraneous substances. I wouldn't die if I didn't satisfy that hunger, but there would be psychological runoff. DNA from the actual skywhale was used to print my synskin. Based on that DNA, Studio scientists determined the nature of my appetite. My body rejected everything. I just wanted French fries—I dreamed of French fries, mountains of them snowcapped in ketchup and mustard and mayonnaise—but I was limited to underwater provisions. Nothing tasted good. They even tried to feed me an actor whose contract had run out prematurely; binding him at the wrists with heavy chains, burly grips made Carmen Adagio walk a plank and throw himself into my tank, but I just watched him sink to the bottom and drown ... By accident, a large patch of strychnine falls into the tank. It had squeezed through the ceiling of the Studio. This happens all the time, but the set is so vast and intricate, groundspeople can't possibly maintain spotlessness at all times, and strychnine grows fast. Thinking it's another bale of poorly constructed sushi, I swim towards it, open my underjaw, and take it in, swallowing without chewing. Immediately I feel sick. I don't vomit. Moments later, I feel energized, euphoric, almost megalomaniacal—with the friendliest and most humane of intentions, I want to break through the glass, stretch my fins, destroy the earth, and dominate the universe. The feeling passes quickly ... Gary the Cervix's lukewarm replacement, Tony the Femur, a name that pays oblique homage to his predecessor rather than signifies his own identity beyond marking him as a different person, stands beside the tank like a sentinel and makes sure nobody strikes the glass. I communicate to him that I want more poison. The doctors not only ensure that strychnine won't kill me, they determine that synskin renders the plant nutritional for me. Psychologists deduce that the druglike effects won't make me physically violent, and by St. Patrick's Day, I am being served four square helpings per day.

Return, or, "History" (Vol. 3). To whom it may concern: Hello! My family immigrated on my mother's side from Germany and knew Lew Wasserman. I grew up in Chicago; ergo, the stalking arrangements were made by Oprah Winfrey, her stepmother Barb, and others via SAG-AFTRA and contract services. Oprah brought in Michelle and Barack Obama. Michelle is from Chicago on the South side, and Barack lived north of the Heights in Pasadena. Together they made the arrangements to pursue me. On multiple occasions, I wrote and called the DA's office, Internal Affairs, and the Grand Jury. Nobody replied. Justice is being obstructed. I want a written reply to acknowledge that they have the information and that I have been turned down for services. Deputies stalked me in the schizoverse and used all methods of tracking, as if I were a criminal wanted dead or alive. They hired actors to mug me, then concealed the evidence. Currently, I am being forced to live in a safehouse among the very men who totaled my car. When I leave the premises, it is obvious that countless pedestrians and bystanders (all of whom clearly have immunity for their actions) have been paid to harass me everywhere I go, day and night. Their task is to break me down. When they succeed, the State will arrest me, confine me to a mental hospital, and drug me—mostly for fun, partly because I chose to talk back. These barbaric, studio-sanctioned practices have been in place for centuries and are supported by all political, legal, law enforcement, and talent agencies. They are carried out through the medium of the entertainment industry so that the victim has no recourse. In addition to my other requests, I have asked for restitution, but so far, society remains pathological, and the collective mental illness that created and facilitates these practices is alive and well. I have given up trying to prove that this is a reverse-racism case. One must always pick one's battles carefully. Best, D.

Edition. Somnambulists recognize the actions of the Vice President, whose sleep patterns have fallen out of synch with consumer predictions. The thirty-sixth edition of *Vice Presidents for Dummies* has not been selling well. The publisher will probably not recoup the funding that went into the edition's production as well as the subsequent book tour that saw the author travel across Europe to conduct signings at his favorite Mediterranean beaches, casinos, and *hôtels de luxe*. Critics agree that the edition offers nothing new beyond a few pithy grammatical revisions and another afterword, which functions more as an extension of the thirty-fifth edition's afterword rather than a stand-alone coda to the book as a whole. Some constituents are asking for the reinstatement of term limits. Hate mail abounds. The Vice President calls a meeting, then boycotts it. Depressed, he retires to his office at the Naval Observatory to smoke a cigar. The humidor is empty. He slumps into a chair beneath the portrait of a beached whale that appears to be deep in meditation as a circle of primates genuflect in worship around it. The portrait's accent light casts eerie, meaningful shadows onto the Vice President's long, troubled face, which rests on his fist like a darkened vase on an ivory pier. We monitor the face, gauging the significance of a chiaroscuro that has yet to bear fruit. Beat. Beat. Slowly the CAMERA PULLS OUT until the Vice President's features disappear into an angular silhouette. Beat.

Stockholm. Doctor Reverend Donovan Ogg Esquire says, "This isn't some casual, run-of-the-mill Attic tragedy. I'm an innovator, goddamn it. Even what's dead and gone can be improved upon and made New." As he assaults the prop designer with a jockey whip, he's careful to leave welts without drawing blood. Everybody watches pensively. Dr. Ogg says, "I don't care what your names are. If I'm looking at you and I call you Bob, or Wanda, or Wonderbread, or Hey You, or Dick Licker, or whatever, that's your name. If you think you're a method actor or some shit and I get word that you want to be referred to by your character name—*I'll kill you*. Method acting? Grow up. Isn't that right, Fish?" I'm sleeping and don't hear him. Dr. Ogg says, "Now then. I understand that most of you are showing early signs of Stockholm syndrome. That's good, but not good enough. I'm holding all of you hostage to the Man. Every one of you dummies should want to fuck me by now. Your psychological alliance with my Bullshit is an inevitable matter of course. Even the termites in the walls believe in my humanity. Ha!" Nobody laughs. Dr. Ogg tells the prop designer to stop crying and put on his shirt. He says, "Look, it could be a lot worse. Have any of you ever worked with Ira Überstein? He's a right cunt and you all know it. Comparatively I'm a goddamn cakewalk." A few crew members nod in agreement. Dr. Ogg says, "Listen, if you don't want to fuck me, just pretend that you do. Right? That's all I'm asking. Okay? You know I'm big on pretending. What people actually *think*, what people actually *feel*, what people actually *want*, let alone what they *dream*—none of this matters at all."

Fourth, or, "Memory" (Vol. 1). In my first memory, I appear in an aquarium. It is almost time to die ... I never want to give up my gills, which is more than I can say for my ghost. Humanity needs the wisdom of my misanthropy, but people will be better off without me. We are all stardust, and to the presolar granary we shall return ... "Skin is the body's overpriced Halloween costume," my surrogate father assures me, regarding me with that cold, amphibious eye. "Only allow it to eat you after the credits roll." Enlightened and authorized, I molt my skin and expose my bowels to the sun ... Water beads on my epithelial tissues, which glint like crystals; passersby need to shield their eyes ... In time, the cleanup crew dumps my remnants into a sewer. I coagulate, follow the runoff all the way to the Abyssinian Sea, and float onto a trench floor. The memory ends here.

Fostoria. Demented, I receive an honorary doctorate degree from Fostoria University, a small liberal arts college in northwestern Ohio. I completed my B.A. at Fostoria almost three decades ago. The ceremony takes place in the Old Gym. Onstage the president welcomes students, faculty, and staff, then introduces me as "Doctor Reverend Donald Ennui Esquire." I take the microphone and correct her. The subsequent acceptance speech is a sixty-minute invective during which I address a variety of subjects, namely the Apollonian state of contemporary filmmaking, the audience's dumb-looking expressions, the atrocity of canned vegetables, and how sex isn't worth the price of admission to having a relationship with a woman. There's a pinch of strychnine in my underlip, and I pause every minute or so to spit in an empty beer can. Otherwise the invective issues from my mouth like a steep mountain stream, fluid and unrelenting, controlled and steady yet furious. I don't pay attention to the words. Rather, my thoughts drift back to Strychnine Heights ... The painted buildings. The bright green trees and shrubbery. The narrow, cobblestone streets that wind through the oneiric tarns and fells. More like Copenhagen than Copenhagen itself. In my daydream, I seek out the tallest hills and briskly march up and down the sidewalks and footpaths, breathing in the pure, unfiltered, rarified air, pausing to admire the clouds in the sky, the architectures in the bedrock, the turquoise ocean in the abyss ... It's a simple, almost banal reverie. It means everything. I belong here, and I am here, always, no matter where I am, or who or what I am. When I'm gone, I crave the Heights, not knowing why, never knowing why. I craved it before I was born, and my desire is my bond. For me, this is Square One and the End of the Line. When I die, they will entomb me in my own statue. Currently it stands on the corner of Pain Avenue and Hog Boulevard, where I shot scenes for *The Valley of One*. I am rust-proof. I am the size of a biblical terrorist. In one light, I am a force of nature; in another, a monster of culture. I am, above all, literally and otherwise, myself. And there is only one of me. And there will be plenty of room for my bones to rot in my effigy.

Pop. In the real world, whales suddenly, inexplicably surge in popularity. This is before the production of *Ambergris* and The Event that sparked its conception. The topic surfaces on the waters of the Collective Unconscious, then emerges in the Media with the same frequency as it is discussed on the streets and in the schizoverse. Within 24 hours, the topic loses steam ... except in Strychnine Heights. Talking about whales seems to empower and invigorate residents, who momentarily forget about the everyday anxieties that harrow them, ranging from the smallest apprehension (e.g., germs) to the greatest fear (i.e., Death). This epistemological riff, this spontaneous combustion of knowledge and power traumatizes objective reality. As such, bruises flower onto the skin of subjective perception. Some of the bruises never go away; the interior bleeds like an eon. The time of whales is long gone, after all.

Peptalk. "People are dying who have never died before in their entire life," says the Studio's stand-in pope during a Take-5 Prayer. "What kind of world have we made in our graven image? The purpose of death is rebirth. All these singularities, all this nothingness—are we really so strange?" Sound of gunfire.

Glitch. Recent stories claim that I have been acting out in the real world like a human being rather than shooting a film in the form of an *Ungeziefer verwandelt*. My first sighting occurs in Florida at the Clevelander Bar where I allegedly slap a man named Gary Indiana (no relation to the singer) at a birthday party. Police question me but do not arrest me once I apologize and invite Indiana out to dinner. Another sighting places me at a yoga studio in Madison,

Wisconsin. After a pranayama class, I shoplift trinkets from a gift store, aided and abetted by a booze-fueled entourage, one of whom mistakenly knocks over a five-thousand-dollar chakra crystal, shattering it. Staffers catch me on tape and turn me in, but authorities fail to apprehend me, and by lunchtime, the robbery has blown over, usurped by more impactful trivia. Two days later I am simultaneously mediating a peace agreement with a minor Animist dictator in Burkina Faso, the Switzerland of West Africa, and dancing with supermodels on a pussy yacht in the Arabian Sea off the coast of Muscat, Oman. In a live interview broadcast, I inform the Vice President of my concerted decision to, first, fall in love with myself, and second, to marry myself. And so on. All of these stories border on the ridiculous, if not in and of themselves, then in terms of my present condition and confinement. A random sample of my DNA could easily prove who, what, and where I am at any given moment. Alas, the general public always prefers the impossible to the unreal.

Numbers. Names of Golden Age stuntmen: Vic Armstrong, Buff Brady, Bob Bralver, Roger Creed, Dick Crockett, Frankie Darro, Babe Defreest, Duke Green, Billy Hank Hooker, Buster Keaton, Eddie Kidd, Bert LeBaron, Jock Mahoney, Bronco McLoughlin, Eddie Polo, Dar Robinson, Guy Teague, Buddy Van Horn, Dale Van Sickel, Dick Warlock ... Ways Golden Age stuntmen accidentally die: fall out of aircraft, fall off roof, fall off bridge, fall off cliff, drive off cliff, get shot, get stabbed, get dragged by horse, get mauled by bear, get kicked by ostrich, explode, burn up, drown, contract staph infection, get beheaded by helicopter blade, get beheaded by samurai sword, dissolve in acid pool, step on active land mine, break neck, suffocate, concuss, electrocute, choke, get trampled by elephants, get run over by train, get crushed by hydraulic compactor, depixilate, sink in quicksand, freeze ...

Describe. It's no secret: meteorologists love it when tornados murder people. Consider the enthusiasm with which Dale Rigueur describes the latest aftermath. (Mind you, this is long before Rigueur becomes the morning anchor for Thirty-Third and Third

News—before Rigueur is *de rigueur*, so to speak, which is to say before he becomes *himself*.) He looks like he has just taken a bite of an award-winning pie as he catalogs the scene's gruesome details, relishing the carnage with his expression and posture as much as his tone of voice. He stands on the perimeter of a soaring concrete bridge beneath which people weep in despair as they wander through the debris and wreckage of their homes. Occasionally they encounter the dead bodies of loved ones and scream uncontrollably. "The devastation is palpable," ejaculates Rigueur. "Ladies and gentlemen, believe me when I tell you that I smell the fear of death. I can almost taste the salt in the tears of these devastated survivors. Who can say if they will ever recover? Nature has lashed out and the consequences are truly devastating. I'm Dale Rigueur." He pauses so that the bass player has time to catch up, but there is a fundamental disconnect between the two, and the percussionists' cymbals aren't getting along together. All told, the weather report's soundtrack needs improvement. Viewers have already started to dream of a hero. Is this a battle that Dale Rigueur should pick with the showrunner? The only thing worse than picking the wrong battle is thinking the war can be won.

Herzog. Werner Herzog threatens to murder Klaus Kinski on a regular basis, but he only attempts to carry it out when the famous director collaborates with the infamous arch-actor. They made five films together. Kinski is to Herzog as Stewart is to Hitchcock, Wayne to Ford, Depp to Burton, Lassiter to Amino, Hanks to Howard, Ennui to Ogg, De Niro and DiCaprio to Scorsese. Short-tempered, controversial, spastic, megalomaniacal, outspoken, unpredictable, and probably bipolar, Kinski terrorizes everybody he works with on set, throws tantrums for hours at a time, and assaults fellow actors, once shooting off an extra's finger. He hates everybody with equal rancor, and he never knows his lines. Audiences love to watch him rant and rave at them. Herzog and his crew members are another story. During the making of *Fitzcarraldo*, Herzog tries to burn down his house as he sleeps, but the arch-actor's Alsatian shepherd thwarts him; on another occasion, a tribe of Peruvian Indians, confused by Kinski's self-stylized antics, ask Herzog if he wants them to "solve" the Kinski problem, and while the director considers the offer, he decides against it. The last film Herzog makes with Kinski is *Cobra Verde*. After that, Herzog liberates himself from the arch-actor's tyranny. Kinski writes his entire autobiography in the present tense, as if to decree himself timeless. Three years after it is published, he dies of a massive heart attack at his home in Lagunitas, California. Sources say he is cremated and dumped in the Pacific Ocean. In reality, he is buried in an unassuming cemetery near his place of birth in Sopot, Poland. Etched onto his tombstone is something he told Herzog whenever he took the camera off of him: "The only fascinating landscape on this earth is the human face." Herzog simultaneously regrets trying to murder Kinski and failing to murder Kinski. "Every gray hair on my head is named 'Kinski,'" laments Herzog, "but, you know, he was one of the few people I ever learned anything from."

Abandon. Meanwhile, I have kidnapped a prominent Third World dignitary and demanded that the United Nations pay ransom. I am straddling the Arc de Triomphe with thighs like California redwoods, and I lay out my platform with the force and resolve of Godzilla's copyrighted screech. The buzzards that dart about my head outnumber the spectators that point and gasp at me in terror. Later, drinking coffee at a diner in Idaho City, a drywall installer attacks me, not knowing that I have been trained by the best Studio-chartered sensei. There are only a few seconds of concrete violence, as with most non-diegetic skirmishes. Earlier, my therapist's secretary interrogates me about the frequency of my appointments. She suggests that I supplement (or altogether surrogate) schizoanalysis with a strain of Cajun edibles. They resemble 8-bit turnips. Fingering her brown neck, the secretary offers me a sample bag and says that they work best when ingested virtually. By nightfall, the gorges and archipelagos of my psyche come to bear like alien predators in a vacuum; only nonsense can save me now. In due course, I remember who I am, discover who I am not, determine who I want to be, and guard against who I might become. This is how we acquire knowledge. The best way to learn something is to watch somebody else fail to absorb it.

Hajime. The link may be defective. They skimped on telereceptors, breaking the triumviral rule of thumb: never skimp on toilet paper, fitness equipment, synskin, or telereceptors. But I can still hear the actors quarreling outside the tank. Doctor Reverend Donovan Ogg Esquire has gotten drunk again. He can only work until 1 p.m. at the latest; then he freely, politely admits to being intoxicated and wraps for the day. Slumped in a foldout lawn chair, he observes the behind-the-scenes action with his trademark gaze, two crimson flames smoldering above the ashes of a sharp white beard. I don't know how the argument starts. As always, my awareness enters the ring *in medias res*. There's an exchange of derogatory remarks as Veronica Yen calls Cory Finger's attitude into question. Then he punches her in the stomach with a hard, no-nonsense jab. Like all actors, they're both duly trained in aikido, Shōtōkan, wuxia, gunkata, and Jeet Kune Do, but she's a much better fighter than him, and as she doubles over from the unsportsmanlike blow, her leg kicks up from behind and she plants a heel in his eye socket with perfect form, like a scorpion stinging prey. During the subsequent fracas, Yen and Finger swear uncreatively at one another as they roll across the floor and fly through the air, crew members and agents and bodyguards and dieticians and security guards and low-level producers taking bets on who will win and who might die. In the end, Yen and Finger become romantic, kissing and groping one another in front of the boisterous crowd with bleeding mouths and broken bones. It's almost like a scene from a movie.

Beauty. I don't recall how much time has passed since my last thought. The thought may have persisted for seconds, hours, days, months ... What comes after a month? No matter. Truth doesn't care about time. Truth only cares about its own existence, which speaks for itself. The lights dim on and off. Every new day brings a new scene, and every new scene produces new emotions, new ways of seeing, new actions and reactions. I am a sick fish. I have the brain of a worm. I can feel my consciousness thrumming in the fibers and tissues of my skin. My memory, on the other hand, lives in a faraway organ ... I am hungry. I am always hungry. Strychnine constitutes the main portion of my diet now. They harvest it from

the Heights and haul it to the Studio every morning in 40-foot con-
tainers. This can't go on forever. One day there will be no more
strychnine left. The Heights will lose its identity to my stomachs. I
have the same number of stomachs as the skywhale: sixteen. That's
twelve more than a sperm whale. They clamor like machines when
they process my intake. I have also agreed to eat domesticated
animals. Nothing wild. Sometimes the feeders try to slip me a herd
of deer or yak, but I can tell. Once they dumped Orestes Dirge into
my tank. He played King Kong in *Carnival of the Barbarians* and
never went back, but I don't eat people, regardless of what they
have become. I keep reminding them. Monsters are still people.
How quickly everybody forgets.

Aside. Have you ever visited a department store? Take down the
exit signs and replace the restroom signs with them. Vice versa. The
result is total mayhem. When shoppers walk through a door, expect
to see a lattice of parking spaces, and discover a row of toilet stalls
instead, they devolve into subhumans. In the opposite case, there
are bladders and bowels to consider; greater difficulties ensue.
There is no time to manage expectations. Civilization is as fragile as
a robin's egg. Touch it—and you taint it. The mother will sense your
deviled imprint, throw the egg out of the nest, and do everything in
her power to demolish it so that nothing bad is born.

Truth. This is not the origin of the species. Nor the terminus. Charles
Darwin's theory of evolution and Tiffany Anaconda's concept of
endtimes have little to do with it. Remember: monsters used to
rule the world, and if anything, the current iteration of sapiens lacks
the gumption to chew on the wind ... The lights continue to dim on
and off. It's not me. My consciousness remains stable, steady, and
functional. I can't blink. I don't have eyelids or eyelashes. In their
place, microscopic gland-bots constantly swim across the surface
of my eyeballs filtering out irritants and foreign material with an
oily protein. This is basically what happens in a real whale, only
the gland is built-in, organic, like the web-shooters on Sam Raimi's
Spider-Man. I am a post-Raimi Spider-Man: technology dictates
the flows of my extensions ... I have no concept of day and night.

I stopped sleeping a long time ago. The consequential deliria now scaffold my reality—which may be completely oneiric, but whether I am always asleep and dreaming or always awake and hallucinating produces the same results in terms of my cognition, my perception, and my ability to do my job ... Hello. I can see you. I can hear you. The glass is clear and my receptors are tuned. You're preparing for another take. You're angry. You're trying not to show it, but there is a hint of spleen in your voice, and your facial tics have given you away. The director insists on multiple takes per scene. This will be your twenty-second take. He insists that you remain nude, even during breaks. You are not an object. He wants you. He repulses you. Didn't he threaten to deport your parents if you failed to abide by his every command, on and off camera? You are not a whore. You are not like the others, ordinary and disposable, just another number. You are, in a word, exceptional—much more than a media sensation or a new-age Aspasia ... Something must be done. I am attracted to you, you see. I can protect you, as it were. I want you. Look at me. Look at me. Watch. I can make my dorsal fin curl into a fist ...

Hermeneutics. NOTHING INCITES TERROR AND EUPHORIA LIKE AMBIGUITY. This so-called "mad maxim" spans the length of Donny Ennui's ulna. Author unknown. It sounds like Shakespeare, but it could just as well be a Mad Lib. Some fans think Donny Ennui wrote it himself, denying that its semantic hammer belies the semblance of its fragile anvil. One encounters the aphorism everywhere in the schizoverse—from the Hallways of Fostoria to the Winter-mute Perimeter—but the first documented sighting traces back to the stillborn megacelebrity's arm. Since then, riffs, allusions, and bootlegs have materialized across every stretch of flesh, psyche, and culture. Unapologetic plagiarism is more common. The first manned shuttle to Venus, for instance, was called the *S.S. Ambiguity*, distinguished by pointillist impressions of the words TERROR and EUPHORIA variously inscribed across the hull and central turbine. What the proverb actually means has been a subject of great debate. On the surface, it appears simple enough: not knowing something—the answer to an equation, what happens to a protagonist in an open-ended novel, whether or not a woman or man you have fallen in love with also loves you, the odds of there being an afterlife or nothingness, etc.—produces feelings of fear and excitement. Humankind's foremost enemy, subjectivity, problematizes the meaning. Doubtless Ferdinand Kovich, for one, is neither frightened nor excited by the same ambiguities as, say, Miriam Shay. In other words, there is no room for individuality or one-sidedness in the semiological meat of Donny Ennui's text, which signifies a purely objective response that pinpoints two extremes on the spectrum of emotions. What about the innumerable emotions that fall between those extremes? I know for certain that Wiley Rant is apathetic about everything. Nothing scares him, nothing throws him a fever-pitch; he just doesn't give a shit about anything. Hence the text doesn't apply to him. And yet, by default, the text infers that it applies to everybody. Or does it? It does. The syntactic placement of AMBIGUITY renders it universal. AMBIGUITY, as it stands, could only refer to a singular, individuated, unique phenomenon in an alternate universe or dimension that operates according to different linguistic cause-and-effect schemas. Here, on earth, in this universe, in this half-ass dimension, the human condition adheres to the laws of science—which, like everything, only exist through the vehicle of language. We are nothing without language. Language structures every aspect of perception, cognition, and civilization as we know it. All of us are word-cyborgs. Excise the word and the noosphere follows suit. So does *Dasein*. Only ennui—the *real* ennui—lingers. Of course, this line of flight enters a phantom zone when we consider the maxim that spans the length of Donny Ennui's opposing ulna: THE ONLY THING WORSE THAN A BAD EGG IS A SHITTY PICKLE. Now we must reassess the meaning of the former text in connection with the latter as well as their combined relation to the fleshly referent on which they appear, as their appearance on other referents, together and *sola scriptura*, will affect their respective connotations, depending on who, what, and where the referents may be ...

Oneirics. Many recent works of reality criticism have centered on how metaphysics originates in dreams, which, for early sapiens, introduced a dynamic that still catalyzes society and culture today. The realization of dreams ruptured consciousness. Sharpened by the whetstone of cognition, primordial beings suddenly saw two worlds, one real and tangible, the other ethereal and spiritual. Without dreams (i.e., without a *self-awareness* of the narratives that unfold across the mind's screen during sleep), the world would not have broken into two parts. Nor would we levy credence in every imaginable direction, including the belief in ghosts and gods that, via religion, has led to more bloodshed than any other pathology in human history. We are only human because we are psychotic. The best we can do is hope that the camera catches our good side in the right light.

Faster. *The Space Race* is a product of *The Cold War*, which is set in Late Reality and depicts a muted conflict between the Soviet Union and the United States. Rooted in *The Nuclear Arms Race*, *The Cold War* begins in 1955 LR with announcements from both countries that artificial satellites will be sent to the moon. The Russians win the inaugural battles, launching the first satellite and then the first human into orbit, but the Americans win the war, landing the first men on the moon in 1969 LR. *The Second Space Race* to Mars unfolds in a similar way, only it takes much longer and involves a war between corporations rather than nations. After Mars, nobody cares about the other planets or even Jupiter's habitable moons; filmgoers set their eyes on the nearest black hole, which is renamed Room 237 in 2080 LR on the 100th anniversary of *The Shining*, and *Space Race III* is on. The picture loses steam quickly. At the time, rockets can only travel so fast. It will take 300 years to reach the gravitational anomaly. Solar radiation wipes out preliminary expeditions before they even make it past the orbit of Neptune. The latest crew passed Neptune six years ago without incident and is expected to arrive at R237 in 678 AR. Beginning in the 90s, the ascendant demographic turns its attention inward with greater resolve and fiscal abandon than ever before. In the aptly titled *Space Race IV: Innerspace*, technopreneurial upstart Baron Caulfield outsmarts his competitors and unbridles the schizoverse, the first all-inclusive mind-body interface, a virtual surreality, a cyberspatial interzone largely derived from science fiction, erotic, and psychedelic literature. Reality suffers the consequences. There is a brief exploration of the boulevards and *canali* of the after-life before the schizophrenic elite realize that reality needs to be reclaimed (and thus reexplored) in some capacity; failure to do so might jeopardize ratings and target audiences. This is still a work in progress, and perhaps a work in futility: reality as we know it (i.e., as we remember it) has proven to be nearly impossible to adapt into a film.

Midnight. I can feel myself inside of myself ... like Jonah, who lives in the belly of a whale for three days and nights. Then the whale vomits his half-digested body onto a beach. The absurdism of the fable solarizes an identity that threatens to swallow me whole.

Oink. There are many unwritten rules of thumb in the Industry. Among the most obvious is that the first scene of every film must involve minor antagonists being fed to half-starved pigs. No excep-tions. What happens afterwards doesn't matter. Ultraviolence vis-à-vis homicidal swine always stimulates viewers' endorphins and spikes ratings.

Id. It takes a child to raze a Village: the idiocy of Ignorance, Impulse, and Aggression will be the end of everything. And if the child has a bad temper, it's gonna hurt ... Fiberoptic tendrils constantly inject me with nutrients, vitamins, anti-depressants, mood stabilizers, and recreational drugs, but nothing seems to work except the anti-gens that nullify my sex drive. I feel bad. And mad. And I am increas-ingly agitated and antsy, sometimes frantic, with RLS in every fin, in every pixel of blubber. My ventral pleats fester and ooze pus. My splashguard aches from underuse. My blowhole itches all the time. Divers can never scratch the blowhole enough. Nor can they adequately scrape the barnacles from my underside, which hurts when I loaf on the aquarium floor. The only things that give me comfort are memories of sex. Certain still shots and poses provide the greatest solace. They may have occurred as I viewed them in a mirror or reviewed them on a screen, but I likely just imagined them while being involved in different sexual acts. During a good fuck, my mind always wanders to better fucks that I have had or will have. And I have never had a better-than-good fuck in the moment. Which doesn't exist. The mind despises the present. The mind shits on instantaneity. It only gives us the Were and the Will Be. Last night I dreamt I was a man again. I had a cloaca that bore no eggs. There was a riot and an enraged laborer slashed my left eye with a Ukrainian kolodach. I could still see through the eye. The doctor squawked in horror when I confronted him, claiming that, in the light of the opium den, the wound resembled the Devil's grin. Under these auspices, I still became a Byronic antihero. In another diegesis, sentient Arriflexes and Panavisions scurry beneath swarms of whispering handheld drones and continually shoot scenes from *Ambergris*—the film unfolds and refolds, bustles and combusts and atomizes and coalesces, orbiting me like becoming-planets around a dying sun. I am the unclocked clocktower of this Village Id, this neo-noir funpark that evolved from the Studio's ragged claws. Whatever happens—it happens because of *me*. And I have never been more useless, evacuated, unmanned, lame. This is the way the world works, beginning to end, then back to the beginning, as if there were no end, because there isn't; never. Last image: a cupula in Strychnine Heights, strangled and rusted by the plant. It meant so much to me, that cupula—I romanced the dusty ghosts of Gretel Marcuse, Krysta Now, Liz Taylor, Marilyn Monroe, and Sarah Bernhardt in its limitless innerspace, breaking them down before firing them up—but now it's fading away, glint by glint, all of it, like me, removed from myself by time and *Imago Dei*.

Today. Excessive megalomania. It always happens at this point during the binge/shoot, like clockwork, almost to the day. This morning I call my neighbor a cunt, a prole, and a Heckless What. He looks at me, hurt and despondent, as if he doesn't deserve it. In under a decade I will rule the ocean and the sky like an extinct volcano possessed by the gods.

Stockholm. The wives want to see Curd right now. They demand it. They don't have passes. They don't have rights. There is a hysterical exchange with security officers, many of whom make passes at the unhinged women between takes. Alerted to the disturbance, the Vice President of the United States enters the lobby with a flourish of kazoos. He has curated an oversized moustache that conceals his mouth; only a hint of chin emerges from the hairy flanks. He addresses the wives in a raspy, affected, exaggerated staccato whose subtext abolishes everything he says. The wives urge the Vice President to let them see Curd. He recognizes one of them as Gretel Marcuse and addresses her specifically, losing his accent for a moment. "I only remember getting married once," he explains. "I was drunk, and she was a stranger, but not a teenager. We were in Old Nevada, at a chapel in the Luxor, and a Charles Manson parodist administered the rites. Things have changed, since then. May I kiss you?" He doesn't wait for an answer, and Gretel Marcuse's young, thin, full-lipped face disappears into his homegrown mask. The kiss is loud and sounds ethereal, like a White Lady wandering through tall, brittle grass at night. It frightens the other wives. They don't know what to do. There's nothing they *can* do. The Vice President doesn't stop until he feels that the wives have sufficiently attuned to their powerlessness, at which point they grow docile, all tension evaporating from the lobby, even if the second-in-command looks like a Venus flytrap feeding on prey. A kiss, he knows, is worth its wait in grandeur. And when the cats stop mewing, Curd will have his day ... The Vice President releases Gretel Marcuse and says, "Your great beauty is only undermined by your dire intellect." He sups moisture from the whiskers with his underlip. "Thank you, Mrs. Marcuse. That was nice." Her knees buckle as she retreats into the fold of the harem and, one by one, the security officers collapse into the walls and floor. The Vice President compliments the other wives at length. "The swing of your hips is nothing compared to your canny resolve," he concludes, then personally escorts them into the Studio zoo, each dutiful woman clinging to him like ivy.

Ashes. At first, investors try to call it Arkham Asylum, but copyright lawyers descend on them like biblical locusts. Hoping to tap into the collective unconscious and syphon consumer bioelectricity, they deploy other, lesser-known names (e.g., Brookhaven, Sonnenstein,

Shutter Island, Briar Ridge, the Overlook, Westworld, Dragonfly Lake, the Cabin in the Woods, etc.), but nothing slips by the vigilance of the Law, which forces the stakeholders to settle on something original. It doesn't take. They end up not referring to the facility at all. The first resident to check in, Billy Combs, played a merman in *Swamp Macabre*. With the exception of webbed phalanges, hemorrhoidal lips, and a few defunct gills, his body had more or less devolved to its original state, but the psychological damage done by the synskin was irreparable. That same year, other noteworthy discards join Combs, among them Widget Moon, Franklin Bolanderos, Sherry Interlaken, Quinn Plotinus Smith, and Sanju K., all of whom exist in various states of cognitive and corporeal disarray from playing, respectively, a dinosaur in *West of Eden*, a yeti in *Don't Go Behind the Diner*, a mutant alien princess in *Brideshead Reverted*, a gwoemul in *Breckonridge*, and a "canine kaiju" in *Salt of the Arf*. Tourism doesn't last long enough to maintain the cost of running the facility and compensating staff. The State steps in and decides that broadcasting occasional footage of experiments being performed on patients will be enough to generate funds from advertisements and cult fandom. The vast majority of actors who use synskin end up succumbing to it. For almost a year, the facility runs over capacity. Then the tides even out: no matter what synskin does to actors in the wake of a film, their lifespan significantly decreases, and they either commit suicide or contract a lightning-fast terminal disease. Sometimes the crematorium in the basement is busier than check-in. Neither users nor viewers pause to contemplate why the popularity of and demand for synskin continues to appreciate.

Rodent. Mr. Jack DeLorean VII visits to the Studio. The executive producer has the same nervous disorder as his distant namesake. Twitching and fidgeting, he makes an innocuous comment about the monster zoo. Doctor Reverend Donovan Ogg Esquire replies, "You look like a rodent, asshole. It's your face. It's your teeth and the turn of your lips. And your jawline. And chin. The ears, too. I won't say you look like a rat—that sounds like I'm being a prick for the sake of it. I assure you that's not the case. I've never met a man that looks like a rodent who has not turned out to be a total liar, a hopeless control-freak, a rotten cunt, and a big dummy. Are you trying to fuck me? Are you going to fuck up this picture? This is my picture. I was given complete creative control. It's in my contract. Fuck off, DeLorean. Why are you here? What are you fucking doing? Get out of my world." Taken aback, Mr. DeLorean apologizes. He has no intention of meddling or getting in the way. He just wanted to drop by and say hello. The director stares at him. As the executive producer turns to leave, Dr. Ogg says, "A jerboa. That's what you look like. I think it's your happy, soulless eyes more than anything." Beat. "Jerboa are desert hopping rodents. They're all over Saudi Arabia and Northern Africa. That's not bad. It could be worse. Looking like a jerboa, I mean. They're cute. They're nimble. They're friendly." Beat. "Nonetheless: *rodent.*"

Eraser. Not until the 40s do filmgoers and filmmakers alike realize that zombies are a dumb, dated trope that only persisted for so long because of literary and film critics, who, for centuries, argued that the undead symbolize, satirize, and assess a wealth of social, cultural, psychological, epistemological, metaphysical, and ontological facets of the human condition. Knowing that academics held zombies in such high regard, people who watched zombie movies felt smart; they were incapable of putting the diagnostic pieces together themselves, holding less than zero interest in criticism, which is, for 99.9% of the population, as clear and decipherable as an alien language, but they had heard there was Deep Meaning in the actions of reanimated corpses, and when people watched people getting eaten, they perceived themselves in a much more positive, productive light, as if they were part of some rogue intelligentsia. After the release of *They Call Me Murder Legendre*, however, even the stupidest moon-watchers had had enough. Subsequently, zombies are never seen again in a film. There is even a short-lived effort to erase the figure from cinematic history, with leaders of the cause inciting riots, starting fires, dynamiting tectonic plates, and assassinating prominent directors, celebrities, and studio politicians. As such, the presence of zombies in literature is reduced to books that are only read by their authors—which, after reality, constitutes the bulk of contemporary fiction.

Zen. Curd: "Let me stop you right there. I am by all means a thoroughbred narcissist. Naturally I like it when people talk about me. People talking about me is the anti-noose *par excellence* that keeps me from sprinting to the gallows. One should never talk about me *to* me, however—I do not want to be made to feel like a narcissist to my face, even when the talk is good-intentioned, harmless, idle, and so on, and especially if the talk is flattering, congratulatory, venerable, and all that. A *fête* is only as good as the ass you strap it to." Beat. "One should *think* about me, however—I want to feel the stream of your consciousness vis-à-vis my identity. Moreover, your discourse and facial postures should indicate that you are thinking about me—but not to an excessive degree. Nobody likes an egregious fanatic. Steady now. Everything in moderation ..."

Past, or, "History" (Vol. 4). To whom it may concern: Hello! To date, I have been sexually assaulted 70 times and physically assaulted 138 times. Surrounding me with bad celebrity actors who consistently do me harm is not helping the matter. I am asking for one home of my choice. I also want my car to be replaced and a yearly pension to be determined by my attorney Harvey Seigel. I should have been able to make money in that circle, but the government interfered; hence I deserve a pension and benefits, just like the group that stalked me and forced me into the sex trafficking industry. What is organized stalking? *The deliberate creation of negative experiences in a person's life whereby antagonists unacquainted with the target execute covert attacks (e.g., drugging, poisoning, mob action, and pet mutilation via hired thugs).* Who engages in organized stalking? *These parties can include gangs, government and non-government organizations, slighted dates, and women scorned.* How do people who engage in this practice live with themselves? *Typically, they profess to be involved in some Greater Good while promulgating the idea that the target or targets are essentially "bad."* Why do they do it? *An organized stalker's motive ranges from sheer malice to personal gain; quite often, perpetrators are themselves victims of a deviant herding instinct.* Remember, only a free thinker can see past the rationalizations that underlie a concerted stalk. Perpetrators are usually fixated on the past. Part of the reason they make such a big deal about everyone's backstory has to do with a yearning for someone to care about them. It's a control issue. They magnify negative incidents in a stranger's life. They spread misinformation in an effort to maintain order, publicly labelling the target as unstable, drug addicted, perverted, violent, and a threat to society. The goal is alienation and isolation. Best, D.

Bygone. By the end of the first decade of the twenty-first century, a movie like *The Mask* can no longer be made. Viewers refuse to tolerate that kind of cartoon irrealism. They demand straight-shooting realism from their comic-book diegeses. By the middle of the century, such diegeses usurp culture at large. What used to be real (or irreal, for that matter) becomes a historical artifact, a forgotten language, an equation with no integers or answer—an AR (After Reality). This new metaphysical hammer forges an evolved dramatis personae, one as different from its past self as early Sapiens and Neanderthals. We might as well be aliens now. Whether or not our condition hinges on intellect, indolence, or idiocy will be determined by the gods of another future.

Lomax. It is by accident that Betty Lomax meets Stanley Kubrick, David Lynch, and Werner Herzog at a restaurant in Liverpool. They are reluctant to accept her company. Female directors make them uneasy, commanding suspicion and needling insecurity. She sits at the table without waiting for an invitation and orders a gin rickey. She tells them that she's from the future in spite of her flapper-chic attire, bob, and bee-stung lips, then throws her head over her shoulders and laughs like a specter. Herzog gets drunk. Kubrick stares at her. Lynch chainsmokes nervously. Lomax bums a cigarette from him and says, "Hello! You have all employed parametric narration in your work with some degree of success." CLOSEUP on Kubrick's intense black eyes. "Stan, you used it most effectively in *The Shining*. Dislocating emotion like that is antiquated in its rawest form, but innovations of the technique have opened new ways of thinking about diegetic life." She takes a drag from the cigarette. EXTREME CLOSEUP on the burning ember. "Work is one thing. Life is the same thing. I apply the parametric model to every aspect of my existence. I don't even have to try. Here. Watch me do nothing and alchemize eternity." The restaurant pixilates, falls apart, and implodes into a central point. There is no formal conclusion, no meaningful residue.

Homily. Ogg: "That's exactly what I mean. Like all good films, this picture will be a surface-skin plateau of high art concealing a down-under shithole of mass culture. And by *good* films, I mean *my* films." As he strangles an intern, the flames of Donovan Ogg's trademark gaze crackle and flare. "I have been drunk for some time now. It's not my fault. Once I cross a certain threshold, I can't stop without a formal detox—the DTs have crashed my heart before. Detox takes time, and as everybody knows, time is never on a filmmaker's side. I keep drinking for all of *you*. And for Fish." He kicks the tank, startling me. "My addiction is my gift to you. Everybody that lives always has a job with me. You can count on that." Bellowing, the director pounces on a caterer and bludgeons her to death, gray bile bubbling onto his white chin. "It's true. There aren't many of us left. This goddamn picture is almost finished, but it looks like I'll have to tap into the resurrection fund again. It's okay. There's always more money in the pot than Administration lets on. The good news is that, to date, I have more kills than any other director in history. Believe me. I'm wanted dead or alive by the Thought Police, but they haven't caught me yet. There's too much hype surrounding *Ambergris*." He falls to his knees and almost passes out. He revitalizes himself with a flask of bourbon. "Serial killers are a dime a dozen. I'm not bragging. Plus, this might be the biggest set ever created. We were a cunt hair away from building our own Death Star to shoot on. Jesus Christ! There were over 20,000 extras in the Operation Hello scene. And they all got paid. That's something else, all right. The point is, this is a big fucking shoot and there are a lot more employees available to kill on it. I'm not special. We're all cut from the same moth-eaten cloth." He fires randomly into the crowd with a handgun. Crew members politely fall out of rank, in slow motion, like line-infantry soldiers struck by musket balls. "Well, fuck it. Everything happens for a reason, right? *Wrong.* Everything happens because of *me*. And you. All of us working together for the sake of art. Art is an artifact, a thing of the past that died with the human intellect, but we do what we can. If it weren't for people like us, the world would be nothing but engineers, plumbers, and public servants." Swig of booze. "Right. Somebody feed Fish. We need to get that dumb sonofabitch in the sky by Thursday and he's gotta be alert. Dead monsters are no good to anybody, especially when they cost more than my home in Monaco. Let's go people! *Velocius quam asparagi coquantur!* Amen."

Fifth, or, "Memory" (Vol. 1). The memory ends here ... and comes back to life like an evil orchid, with a roll of kettle drums, resurrected by an editorial loop ... In order to kill history, we need to kill the dreamer. All of the dreamers. In this way, we filter desire from the black hole of futurity and pass into its warm, loving anus ... The memory never ends, then, because there is nothing to remember in the first place.

Blot. I die during principle photography. Nobody notices until strychnine starts to build up in the tank and cloud the water, hiding the mountain of my decomposing corpse. They still do the drop. Special effects antiquarians must digitally graph a screaming mouth and flailing tongue onto the dead, lifeless cavern on my face. Critics and viewers pan the retroaction. Donovan Ogg commits suicide twice during the years-long promotional junket.

Nature. The rustle of trees is overrated. So is the smell of fresh ocean air. The shadow of a distant mountain still holds some clout, but it's nothing compared to a blank sky and a beeline horizon. There hasn't been a wave in weeks. The only ripples in the water form when horseflies and mosquitos land on the surface and drown in the scum. The city behind me beats like a pulsar. I put a conch shell to my ear and it screams like a goat. In fact, the shell is a goat head, severed and tied at the neck. I toss it aside and it rolls across the sky, which falls into a timelapse loop—now we can see how the clouds rorschach into mundane shapes that signify The End. I look away. These plastic clouds are more than mere Petri dishes for my thoughts; they are the universe's quiet carrion, twice removed from my power and resolve. Strewn across the shore as far as the eye can see, beached whales rot beneath the forgotten sun. Decomposing blubber is among the worst smells on earth; its stench transcends the describable, and its impact is corporeal; one vomits or dry-heaves before even breathing it in; in this instance, proximity is stronger than assimilation. The gray bones of a rib cage encircle me like Stonehenge. A liana of strychnine reaches out of the sand, slithers around my forearm, and constricts the flesh, inflating the veins in my wrist and hand. I see a memory in the vascular pattern. It is a one-man show set in the playroom beneath the stairs. My mother used to hide me there when the Turks came for blood. Induced by *Herod the Great*, a lost Shakespearean play recovered by Jacobean archaeologists from a dig in Bishopsgate, they murdered all of the male children in the neighborhood. Only one boy survived the holocaust. He grew up to become a vengeful god, just as the tragicomedy predicts. After he frees the whores and liquidates the elders, he retreats to the Lake District to dress his wounds. The landscape of the region rivals the layout of his psyche. Beyond this cue, there is no concrete description in the screenplay; readers must conjure the vista themselves. Curd used to enjoy this practice when he was a young man full of ambition and positivity, when every failure instantly became a new learning experience, a hopeful challenge, another excuse for rebirth. Now he has been reborn too many times to care, remember, or shirk his redundancy. He is a docile robot. He is a mechanical object, subject to the clockwork that usurped his dead soul. This is neither unexpected nor unique. What happened to him happens to everybody: born a vegetable, become a monkey, die a machine.

Heliocentrism. I can't remember my line. "Prithee," I say. The DSM says, "Born a vegetable, become a monkey, die a machine." I hear him, but it doesn't register: I forget the line before I remember it. "Prithee," I repeat. The DSM says, "Born a vegetable, become a monkey, die a machine." I think about it. "That line's horseshit," I say. "Like, the syntax is fucked up. Give me another line. I'm not saying that bullshit, you fuckin' dummy." The DSM says, "Born a vegetable, become a monk—" I attack the DSM. He's bigger than me and uses his height and weight to his advantage, but I'm too fast, and my training is wholly automated; all I need to do is decide to destroy somebody and my neurons take care of the rest. I break the DSM's arm and wound at least ten stagehands that come to his aid. I knock out a rigger with one punch, dislocating his jaw. Everybody gets mad at me. I don't apologize—I never apologize—I blame them for not being on their toes, for being out of shape, for lacking fighting experience, sharper reflexes, and better genes. I feel badly for the crew. It's more sympathy than empathy. Perhaps only sympathy. They know who I am and they know what to expect, but it's hard to be an insect, no matter how aware you are of the giant that stomps on you. The ASM replaces the DSM. We backtrack and repeat the last scene. Several minutes later I can't remember the line again. The same thing happens, only I kill the ASM. To prove a point, the Studio has me fined, arrested, and released on bail, all in the same breath; in the next breath, my lawyer makes them pay the fine and the bail. I still can't remember the line. My therapist looks at the script and reads it aloud to me: "Born a vegetable, become a monkey, die a machine." I say, "You sound like the goddamn Vice President of the United States, reading that." We talk about the rumors surrounding the Vice President, how he's an imposter, a simulacrum, my father, me, my surrogate, etc. I describe another dream and we dissect it. The next day, I remember the line, but I refuse to deliver it. Standing off-camera, my therapist heckles me, calling me loaded names, telling me I'm a product of culture, and threatening my alpha-masculinity. I lose track of time. There's another fight during which I scream, "Prithee! Prithee! Prithee!" at nobody in particular. Later, sidetracked by a chain-reaction of bad memories, I hear myself utter the line. I have come full circle. The last thing I hear is my heart powering off like a turbine.

Loss. "When you smile," says Donny Ennui, "your gums are longer than your teeth." Elizabeth Partwater resents the legendary prestidigitator's footnote, although he doesn't enunciate it with any malice in his tone, posture, or expression, and he genuinely seems to love her. Nonetheless she finds herself at the liquor store later that afternoon. If she gets wine, she can last longer before getting too drunk to function; if she gets gin, she'll feel better quicker, but she'll get drunker quicker ... She gets gin. And wine. And some other necessities. She mixes and consumes several cocktails in the parking lot, then brings a bottle back to Donny Ennui's rental estate in one of the Heights' prestigious hillside neighborhoods. She can't locate him, and the gardeners don't speak Spanish. She almost falls in the pool before vomiting in the gazebo. Refreshed, Elizabeth Partwater nurses the bottle as she wanders through hallways and up and down stairways. She finally discovers Donny Ennui in the basement. He's crouched over a workbench. He appears to be wearing clown makeup. Moving closer, Elizabeth Partwater realizes there's nothing on his face; it's just the lighting. In slowtime, he turns his head and peers over his shoulder at her. Beat. CAMERA MOVES IN to CLOSEUP on his steel-gray eyes. She smiles, becomes wary of her gums, shields her mouth with a hand, and takes a drink. She leans in to kiss him—the angles of his face shift in and out of focus—then pulls away, dizzy, flustered, and hot. She orgasms, emitting a curt moan that is more surprise than delight. She staggers backwards. She dry-heaves. She burps. She smiles. She presses her lips together to conceal the smile ... Donny Ennui observes her like an ape in a cage. He wonders if she's here to kill him. Who is she? He doesn't know her. He doesn't even know himself. Is he currently in character? Who is he? Where is he? What is he doing, literally? He looks down at his hands, his lap. He looks inward and searches through the index of recent memory. Nothing. "Take off your clothes," he tells Elizabeth Partwater. "That outfit makes you look like an emaciated pig. If you get naked, you'll just look like a pig." As she struggles to oblige him, she gets tangled in her jeans, which are too tight, with too many zippers and deviations. In the meantime, Donny Ennui's thoughts float across the sky like constipated clouds. Rumpled and dark, they want to rain but can only produce meek bursts of dry, corked thunder.

Wake. Preparation for the first screening takes considerable time and manpower. Thereafter it is simply a matter of tweaking minor details. A different demographic of mourners attends each event. Undertakers change the body's clothes and rearrange its facial expression depending upon the demographic's collective memory and desire. The idea is to create a sense of familiarity via reflexivity, if not peace, love, and "happiness." Masseuses amble through the mortuary and rub people's shoulders; there are massage chairs for anybody who doesn't want to be touched and sex booths for everybody who wants more than they deserve. Appetizers are limited yet mouthwatering and stylish. The bar is open, fully stocked, labyrinthine, and impossible: it angles across every floor, wall, and ceiling of the mortuary, defying gravity and the acausal laws of reality, with bartenders politely standing sideways and upside-down, ready to serve anybody who can reach them. Shockingly, not one fight breaks out all day, and the police only show up twice to give parking tickets and mace strangers. The Vice President of the United States is nowhere to be seen. After the final screening, interns remove all clothes from the body, spread petals of government-issue strychnine around the coffin, close the coffin, and deliver it to a storage facility where cameras installed on the interior of the lid will film the decomposition process. In eight to twelve years, timelapse footage of the process will be broadcast around the world and marketed with respect to the social and cultural climate of that not-too-distant future.

Recurrence. They resurrect me for the third wave of post-release promotions. I have no concept of time, and I don't know who or what or where I am. And yet I have something to say. I say: "If I'm nice to you, it's only because I want to fuck you. There's no other reason. More to the point, soft drinks hurt. They're abrasive on my throat. They're not soft. They're, like, hard. I don't know who named them soft. Any other questions?" I observe the audience with a sleepy eye. Somebody raises a hand and says: "What was Melville like? Was he a good guy? Was he gay?" I blink the eye. "I don't know what he was like. All I did was read *Moby Dick* a thousand times and interview a simulacrum of the author manufactured by a Melville-specific word virus. The simulacrum lacked the real Melville's social and cultural construction, of course, and I didn't ask it anything about its sexuality. I think he was gay. Weren't they all? Isn't everybody?" No response. I say: "Well, thanks for coming out. The movie will premier in early September. Principal photography is over, but there's still a lot to do. Doctors say they'll start to ungrow me the day we wrap, but they don't know how long it'll take to reiterate my core. There's always the chance it won't work and I'll be stuck this way. It's not so bad. I can always kill myself, right? Cheers." But I have already been ungrown. I'm not here. I'm mist. I'm ether. I'm memory. Pure memory, utterly intangible, pitiably real ... In the past, which is the future, I'm floating in a rollaway aquarium with a great bundle of Strychnine lodged in my underlip like chewing tobacco. I'm speaking via telepathic receptors that broadcast my thought-responses across the newsroom. I'm nauseous and have to empty my bowels, but I hate swimming in my own dirt. I've never been this lonely. I've never felt this suicidal. I begin to cry as my entourage pushes me out of the room. I don't mind swimming in my own tears.

Bonaparte. Look at the expression on Donny Ennui's face. Now read the expression, analyze it, and construct an operable hypothesis in connection wtih the universe. Pull out. Sweat stains have spread from the illustrious raconteur's armpits onto the undercurve of his pectoral swoop, yet he carries himself with a relaxed awareness, fingers and limbs synched with the inflections of his careful eyes and nimble speech patterns. He's presenting a lecture to a group of college students. Fostoria University hires him once a year to teach a masterclass in Reality Studies over the span of a fortnight. Note the subject matter—how it deviates from the course description in the syllabus, how it violates university policy and at least two constitutional amendments, how it only makes sense within the context of a certain rubric, at a certain time of year, in a certain ambiguous, embryonic light ... The film under discussion has been banned in 203 countries and retitled on four occasions, all of which occurred during the Hot Scare and the brief reign of Yellow Mike. Currently the title exists in a volatile, amorphous state, like celluloid on fire. Look at the students that populate the rows of the lecture hall. Is that genuine or simulated attention? What is going on in their heads? It doesn't matter. Donny Ennui makes no bones about it; all he requires is their gaze—if their thoughts drift elsewhere, so be it. Halfway through his seventh formal vituperation during which he claims to be a "halfass reincarnation" of Yellow Mike—"as we all are, to varying degrees," he opines—the drone that circles his body like an electron reminds him that both his hygiene and appearance are on the verge of collapse and need immediate refurbishment. "Recovery is not possible without relapse," he communicates to the drone. The drone reminds him that there are no excuses for not living one's best life at all times. Guilted, Donny Ennui removes an electric razor from the inner lapel of his black, sand-worn duster. He begins to shave his chin and cheeks as he paces back and forth across the apron of the stage. Stubble flies into the faces of students in the first three rows. Afraid to react, they try to maintain composure. It's impossible for Fiona Candelabra not to gesticulate, Ned Fix not to sneeze, Augustus August not to dry-heave, and so forth. There are other celebrities in the audience. They sneak in through the exit doors after class has begun and the lights have been dimmed. What is their intent? Why do they care what Donny Ennui has to say about the structure of reality, Yellow Mike, good posture, global hoaxes involving "runaway ice ages," the future of Canada, or anything? None of them are taking notes on paper or screen. Even mental notes are sparse. What's wrong? Are they insane? Where are their bodyguards and agents? Their entourages? Their parents, children, ex-wives, lovers, whores, and slaves? Did they grow up in Canada? Is Canada so bad? What is their net worth, individually and collectively? Are they more popular than me? What is the best way to gauge popularity? Why is dusk reliably more fun than twilight? Which is the myth: subjectivity or objectivity? Are you a has-been, a washout, a dried-up cunt? Am I better than you? Does your Napoleon complex outshine mine? Given the tools, who among us will build another world? More importantly, which one of us will shoot to kill first?

Hello, or, "History" (Vol. 5). To whom it may concern: Hello! In an effort to bring closure to this sequence of traumatic episodes, I will exact a denouement that, ideally, makes me feel better. Closure is subjective—nobody benefits from tying together loose ends but the user. Hence the following catalog of wrong-doings levied against my person. I will be as concise as possible; at this point, even I lack a frame of reference concerning the issue, as if all these things happened to somebody else, in some other time and diegesis, on an alien planet. In short, terrorists have committed the following acts against my life: [1] enslavement; [2] imprisonment or other severe deprivation of physical liberty in violation of the fundamental rules of international law; [3] torture; [4] rape, sexual slavery, enforced prostitution, online stalking, and associating my phone number with lewd copy so that men can take advantage of me; [5] other inhumane acts of a similar character intentionally causing great suffering or severe injury to my mental and physical wellbeing; [6] the totaling of my car; [7] use of illegal informants for political gain; [8] surrounding me with bad celebrity actors that do great harm; [9] hacking my computer, phones, and brain; [10] workplace mobbing; [11] identity theft; and [12] revising history by expunging the future. There's more, and the latter transgression in particular requires concerted unpacking, but anything I say seems to instigate an infinite regression of wordplay, lawsuits, and death sentences. I have repeated myself ad infinitum to boot. At this stage, I can only hope that I get what I want—which, for all intents and purposes, is to be reimbursed, compensated for hardships endured, apologized to, given a new car, and left to my own unburied devices. Best, D.

Goodbye, or, "History" (Vol. 6). To whom it may concern: Hello! I am not a whale. I ceased to exist at Hawgstrüffel Studios in Strychnine Heights, California, on the 12th of January, 542 AR. My father was Doctor Reverend Donovan Ogg Esquire. He taught me how to love him by ignoring me. My maker was a man named Curd. He lived in a tree. He whittled my limbs from bark and used bird droppings to glue together the pieces. These seminal patriarchs have expired more than once. The gods treat the dead like gladiators, but we know the truth: failure lurks around every corner waiting to pounce on another tourist. I used to be a panhandler, an addict, an actor, and an idol. Now they call me Eddy Caledonia. Despite history and memories of over 100,000 alternate personalities, I have never been anybody but myself. I am pale and alive. Never turn your back on the ocean. With sentience comes hurt feelings, and the earth is madder than you think. Every morning I used to drive my car onto the beach and listen to the waves, each of which contains a message from the earth's core. You'd be surprised how much it has to say; most of the dialogue concerns the core being hot, lonely, and overburdened with keeping the earth and its inhabitants animate and healthy. Since they totaled my car, I never go to the beach anymore. I don't really go anywhere. Leaving my condo unsettles me. And if I do leave, I just end up in one of my other condos, running my fingers through the carpet. This is my last hurrumph. The show must *not* go on—for some reason, I have avoided this dead-to-rights thesis as if it were mankind himself. Everybody knows that, if something bad happens, you give up and run away. I have stuck it out for too long, on too many occasions. For my trouble, I have been stalked, spied on, spit on, beaten up, ridiculed, satirized, scapegoated, and molested. Half the time nobody even knows who I am. Including filmmakers. It's not uncommon that directors forget my name, and I'm the star of every show I've appeared in. I give my best performances when I'm antagonized, emasculated, and made to feel small, but this catalyst is Old News and escapes everyone; Lloyd Radar, for example, had no idea what makes me tick, and when he tried to have me arrested for vagrancy and removed from the set of *Freud: The Penultimate Biography*, he was being genuine. It didn't matter that I was in the middle of a scene. In my trailer, I plotted to murder him several times over, but my assistants fed me drugs and talked me down, marveling at my terpsichorean fury. I am not the executor of knee-jerk complaints. My rancor is never without reason. Remember when I leapt off the stage and pummeled that cow in the front row for distracting me by putting her hat in her lap? It was a bad hat, an egregious hat, and she situated it over her private parts in a way that suggested I might look at them. I don't give a shit about her nudity! Later, as I made love to her in the parking lot, I realized that I had found my soul mate. Ultimately she was as toxic and desperate as a studio administrator. I married her. We flew to Lost Vegas and did it in a chapel at the Pequod, strangling each other to death as we said our vows. This might have been years before or after the run of the play. Now I lie in wait for the dramaturges to tell me what to do as my flesh petrifies and dust settles onto the mantle of my bad attitude. I won't say a word or move a muscle unless somebody makes me. I don't care what it stipulates in my contract. And I don't care how long it takes. Forever means nothing to me. Best, D.

Corporeality. For the last time, off-camera synapses flood my mind's screen with memories of who I used to be. The memories are broken and unedited, but not without direction. Some of them actually happened. Most are the residual afterimages of dreams, dress rehearsals, acid tests, and recreational implants. My fingerprints are gone. Only the knuckles on my back and the barnacle scars on my stomach distinguish me. In the end there is only my unrealizable body.

Widow. They don't know what to do with me and they don't want to resurrect me for the long haul. It would be too costly to regress the synskin, whittling me back into something like the man I once was. In addition, my celebrity has run its course. Management builds a cannon large enough to shoot my corpse onto the outskirts of a forest bordering Strychnine Heights. It's a big deal, with lots of media hype, and the Studio recoups the cost of the cannon as well as a good chunk of *Ambergris*'s domestic losses. I rot for months beneath a teal sky. Visitors are particularly taken by my fins, all of which petrify, curled into mountainous fists.

Tempest. The era during which androids replace actors only lasts a few years. People don't want to see non-people acting like people. After the death of reality, protocol doesn't change: no matter what happens, desire rarely diverges from the same bandwidth, which can be traced from the Last to the First Men. This recalls a mnemonic issue. In order to forget somebody, one must first confine them to the Hairy Basement of memory. And yet I am always forgotten before I am remembered—an impossibility, but there I am, sucking filth from the basin of the Abyss like an algae-eater. Enter the schizoverse. At the outset, this innerspatial realm served only admen, sex addicts, and social deviants (i.e., the majority of human beings). It quickly became banal. Users normalized it. They took it for granted, forgot it was there, forgot they were even inside of it … at which point the schizoverse usurped the domains of reality, subjectivity, cognition, and most invasively, the unconscious. Not even the schizoverse knows who's in charge now. The screens of the real don't just watch us. They can see into our heads. They can see our memories and dreams play out on the screens of our imaginations. The human turnstile no longer exists; now there are only screens and the shadowy, back-lit forms behind them. If anybody controls this place, it is chiaroscuro. The vicissitudes of time don't help. Time has fangs. It will strike like a rattler if you step on its tail. Hacking it into pieces will produce greater yet subtler calamities and involve the quiet implosion of spatial relations. Space needs time but time doesn't need space. The movie that depicts this thesis, *Mystery Hill*, was shot in Sandusky, Ohio, near a casino off the coast of Lake Erie. Studio geologists determined that the laws of physics, cause, and effect did not apply to this location, a two-square-mile tract of unassuming farmland. In one scene, I remember walking on the underside of a cloud in my bare feet. It felt like moss on my delicate pink soles—much thicker than in my reveries. I didn't jump out of a plane, and I wasn't strung up on wires or strung out on mushrooms. I don't know how I got up there, but I received the Best Crowdstare Award for the scene, and during the post-promotional comedown, I continued to feel a sense of disjointedness and amnesia, as if that weird cloud had stolen something from me, or poisoned part of my brain. I still feel it today, right now, in this moment. I am here and not here. I am growing older but look at me: I remain the same—static, invariable, terminally affected—a carbon copy of my juvenile self, physically and emotionally. This has nothing to do with objective reality, which died over 500 years ago, shortly after the turn of the thirty-first century. Whether the schizoverse predates or supersedes reality is debatable. We know with some certainty that the catalyst was benign. In all likelihood, the slow coalescence of diegetic "independencies" reached a breaking point and burst asunder, slinging fragments of What Used To Be to the far corners of conceivability. The movie that depicts this event, *Bushleague Pragmatism*, was shot in a parallel universe that demonstrated more metaphysical stability than the content of the project itself; the director had no choice but to use exorbitant special effects, albeit he did so on the sly. Information pertaining to the death of reality was embedded in a monologue I delivered to a whore with whom my character had fallen in love. They cut the monologue at the last minute, deeming it too risqué and ambiguous, but it was retrieved and embedded into a supplementary screen-of-consciousness, and I won the Best Cutout Award. I had been murdered once that morning and died of natural causes twice in the afternoon. I accepted the award posthumously in the guise of the mortician who cremated me on all three occasions. The audience didn't know if I was satirizing life, humanity, myself, or the culture machine that produced me. This uncertainty (or rather, my skillful ability to produce this uncertainty) landed me the Best Award Acceptance Award, which was presented to me as I lurched offstage. After the show, I accidentally got drunk in an alley and reenacted the death of Edgar Allan Poe, exclaiming the Final Words, "Lord, help my poor soul," before keeling over dead for a fourth time within 24 hours. Scattered applause. The lavenders, buskers, urchins, and opium eaters who gathered to watch the performance toasted to my memory as I flickered and evaporated like a hologram. That was then. In realtime, the worn cobblestones and oxidized bricks of the alley come apart, shift, mutate, and reassemble into a futuristic diegesis that wraps around and interpolates my body. I am suspended above a busy interzone, with three bales of strychnine stuffed into my underlip, spitting juice into the nearby bay. I am legless. I am skinless. I am fatality. I am master to my backbone—more of an idea than a monster. Only when I sleep do I exist. Awake, I fall to the earth, crushing buildings, pedestrians, wharfs, and yachts. The pain is ridiculous, impossible. It must be a dream. Hysterical paparazzi scurry up and down the cathedral of my bones and document my evolving gore. Word hordes explode overhead. All of my movies end in verbal fireworks that belie their cybernetic essence. This is the very methodology deployed by the Beastie Boys in every song. Behind the image is chaos; behind the word, a post-vodka bodybuzz. I make no apologies even as producers genuflect to investors, patrons, media moguls, and zero-degree warlords. Avant-reality reviews of existence have been largely sycophantic.

We still don't know if innerspatial regulations are in place. Fixers continue to jones for raw imagination; synthetic provisions can only take them so far. There's a good chance that our subjective functions belong to the Third Party. Everything is as connected as a Buddhist utopia yet as unrelated and displaced as alterity itself. JUMP CUT to the ruins of Strychnine Heights. My blood—only my blood—floats into the sky in terrific globs as if gravity suddenly ignores it. The paparazzi catch it on camera, zooming in and out on the corpuscles. This angular momentum, this systemic armature is not a mere *longue durée* with no expiration date. Trace it back to the cause: my first concerted bowel movement, a remarkable event that poisoned the drinking water and gave everybody in town at least one STD within a matter of hours. Nobody died. This coincided with the day on which cinema took control of reality and became the entropic mortgage it always wanted to be. The best mortgages are the ones that can never be paid off. The reel has usurped the real on at least three historic occasions, however, each of which redefined subjectivity, culture, and society. Degrees of the subsequent ambiviolence inform every decision we make, every glance we cast, every dream that binds us, every monkey that climbs on our back and forces us to be more than we can be.

Oxygen. "The electricity in the clouds has nothing to do with the madness of the sun or the tantrums thrown by the earth's core. These are unrelated emergencies. Whether tomorrow is the corpse of yesterday remains dubious, but a ghost is more plausible than a body" (101,010).

Scene. Curd blinks ... and finds himself in a café. Outside: the red skyscape ... He remembers walking here, but he doesn't know what city he's in, and he can't remember sitting down at a table by the window. He mixes stevia into an espresso with a small spoon. The stranger sitting across the table looks familiar. She smells familiar, too. Her peroxide hair is straight and sharp—the guillotine of fibers that hang above her shoulders looks like it could pierce the skin. He wonders if he slept with her. He wonders if she loves him. Curd says: "I played a Vice President in six movies. In two of the movies,

I was the same Vice President, only at different stages of his life. In the other movies, I played completely different Vice Presidents. Three of the Vice Presidents weren't based on anybody real. One was. I can't remember his name. He wrote a book, though, and they made a movie about it. That wasn't the subject of the movie I was in. I like your top. It's perfect for your breasts. Not too much cleavage. Nor too little." She pulls a six-shooter with an oversized barrel from beneath the table and levels it at Curd's face. He blinks ... and she fires. He feels his ears and jaw fly apart from his head as his nose, eyes, brain, and skull explode against the wall behind him. A nearby waiter gasps. The bartender vomits. Curd says: "You can address me as Mr. Vice President, if you like, but most people call me by my real names. There are a lot of them. I forget who I am sometimes. Don't take it personally. It doesn't mean I don't love you as much as you love me. I don't like to connect with people, but I like to think I'm *capable* of connecting with people. I'm not afraid of meaningful connection." She's having difficulty holding the gun up, especially after the kickback from firing it. She grips it with two hands and fires again, this time at his chest. His back snaps into a question mark, his ribs shoot like tusks in every direction, and his internal organs erupt from his body in an obscene surge. One of his arms falls off. Patrons scream and faint. Curd says: "It all goes back to Donny Ennui. Many of my fans got this idea that he's me. People who hate me think he's definitely me. I can assure you: *Donny Ennui is not me*. He's somebody else. He used to be anyway. He was my campaign manager in the 70s. We had a few good runs. This was before I fell out of the sky and ate the world. He tried to shake me down and I had to let him go, and then my running mate killed him during a rally in a swing state. He beat him with a crowbar in front of the Women's Christian Temperance Union. Those crazy broads just loved it. He had a resurrection clause in his contract, unfortu- nately, and he became an actor. He was even in a few of my films, although I never saw him on set. I keep to myself. I hate leaving my trailer. I'm going to kiss you now. Is that all right?" He is two legs and a broken spine. She twitches and shakes, horrified by what she has done, but determined to see it to the end. She stands and fires again and again into his lap, liquifying it. His spine sinks like a flag into the carnage as his legs slosh onto the floor. There's almost nothing left of him now. He's almost gone. Curd says: "No matter what happens, I want you to know that I never intended for things to end this way. Things should only end the way we intend them to end. Why shouldn't everybody get what they want? That's what I always tell my constituents. This means I lie a lot, but I live for the rare instances of good fortune that allow me to follow through on my promises. We are only as true and good as our incapacity to sustain a lie. You can quote me on that. I said it, after all. I'll include it with my signature, if you like. Do you have a pen? Have you purchased a headshot yet? You can get one fairly cheaply in the Dealer Room. Thank you. I appreciate your attention. I wish there were more extremists like you in this world. I do hope you'll stop by my room later. Here's my key. Wear a garter belt. I prefer crotchless lingerie. I'll be there forever and always, waiting for you."

Orphan. I am no alchemist, but it never takes long to eat myself. Sometimes I don't even know I'm doing it. I'm always hungry and I never get full. After a meal, I enjoy a light swim. I live on a thin artificial lake that feeds into the ocean. I stride to the edge of the pier in my back yard and dive off. The water burns. My skin turns red and catches fire. I swim towards the horizon. My strokes are strong and never waver. Eventually my skin revolts against me. The credits roll upwards into the alien sun. I never want to die, but I don't want to live forever. I keep going. I make it to the ocean, then lose steam. My skin takes me down. Down, down. I clank against the ocean floor like a lead pipe. The glass cracks. Propelled by the lazy motor of a tailfin, I explore the crystal depths and emerge into the aluminum sky. I don't fall. I eat myself again, soaring through exhaust fumes and media clouds. Runoff from orbiting satellites penetrates the atmosphere. It tastes like iodine and filets my throat as I consume the trachea, the esophagus, the larynx, the epiglottis. My stomach digests itself and I fall down. Down, down. I never land. I go deeper and get higher, searching for a feeling that I have never experienced. I don't even know if the feeling exists. I eat myself again. Again. I can see my house from the moon. The sum of my eroded memories doesn't stop me.

Gunplay. They raid the bunker and take everything. The auteur oversees the auction, foregrounding the various autobiographies he has written about himself. Most of the autobiographies are expensive leatherbound editions. One has a carbon-fiber, bullet-proof cover that features an acid-etched self-portrait of the man. None have titles. Pacing throughout the conference room, the auteur informs the buyers that titles have no meaning, inherent or otherwise. "I am beyond titles, in any case," he exclaims. The buyers express concern about the merchandise, perplexed by the auspices under which it was stolen, but I play the right card, and within the hour, nothing goes unsold, unbought, or incommunicado.

Query. Who is Harry Florida? He is *not* Boris Pachulski. For the most part, Sally Code insists that they are the same person, but on four occasions over the span of three years, she has confessed to the media that her claim may be "a perceptual, cognitive, or other-wise mnemonic shortcoming." The actors look exactly alike. They are not androids. They are not twins. They are not related in any way—Studio scientists have tested them repeatedly. And yet they are mirror images of one another, and even the topography of their fingerprints flirts with absolute equality. Realtime cetologist Dr. Otto Dykstra has always wondered if it has something to do with whales. Several critics have gone so far as to suggest that they are roosters in disguise, a contention that neither holds water in reality (i.e., fowl isn't smart enough to roleplay, etc.) nor accounts for their fearsome resemblance (i.e., there are no lookalike roosters that aren't twins, etc.). As the matter stands, it appears that the resem-blance will remain an anomaly forever.

Hello. The president never leaves the Oval Office. When they finally break down the door, he has largely decomposed. Studio scien-tists determine that he has been dead for his entire first term and most of the second. Within the hour, I announce my ascension and foreground my platform: "Hello! I am precisely who you think I am. There's been a lot of talk about my predecessor's policies on ter-rorism. Rest assured, I always negotiate with terrorists, be they real, oneiric, literary, cinematic, or extraterrestrial. This is how I conduct business. First, schedule a Peace Talk with a designated hate-group. Second, kill everybody in the room, then burn the bodies before they can be resurrected on the streets. Third, deny all wrongdoing, and apologize for nothing. Fourth, wait for things to smooth over. Fifth, call another Peace Talk, and repeat. Farewell and God be with you, my dear good friends."

Sixth, or, "Memory" (Vol. 1). In my first memory, I appear in my last memory. I know something's wrong. It's bedtime. My parents are dead. Everybody's dead. There's nobody to talk to about dying in my sleep. There's nobody to tell me what to do, to say, or to think. The flame of the lamp on the nightstand moves back and forth, slowly, like a strand of kelp in an underwater forest. I enjoy my pajamas—they're comfortable, stylish, and fit just right. I brush my teeth. I wash my hands and face. I pray for something, anything, then get into my coffin, close the lid, and prepare for action. One take. No costume changes or reshoots. No pressure. The memory ends here.

BIBLIOGRAPHY

Used. Herman Melville. *Moby Dick; or, The Whale*. 1851 LR (Late Reality). Anti-Oedipus Press, 2320 AD (After Donny). From Vitruvian Entertainment via the Atrocity Agency: Copyright © 542 AR (After Reality) by Hawgstrüffel Studios and Stick Figure, Inc. Extrapolated by permission. All rights unnerved.

Simon Duric. "The Filmmaker." Hawgstrüffel Studios, 2003.

OTHER TITLES BY RAW DOG SCREAMING PRESS

A CONGREGATION OF JACKALS
S. Craig Zahler

A MIRACLE OF RARE DESIGN
Mike Resnick

AND YOUR POINT IS?
Steve Aylett

ANTI-TWITTER
Harold Jaffe

ISABEL BURNING
Donna Lynch

LAST BURN IN HELL
John Edward Lawson

ON QUIET NIGHTS
Till Lindemann

PLAY DEAD
Michael A. Arnzen

SOFT APOCALYPSES
Lucy A. Snyder

SPIDER PIE
Alyssa Strurgill

THE MAN WHO LOVED ALIEN LANDSCAPES
Albert Wendland

WELCOME TO OAKLAND
Eric Miles Williamson

Outré